Hi READER

Home for Christmas

JAN RUTH

This book was given to me
by the Author. If you enjoy these
Short stories please read her
other Novels. They are excellent
I have read every one, and cannot
wait for her next one.

Jenny RILEY - OWEN

(N.B. Life of RILEY)

X

P.S. They can be downloaded on Amazon to.
KINDLE

Contents

Rudolph The Brown-Nosed Reindeer

*Rick isn't looking forward to his lonely corporate Christmas,
but it's the season of goodwill, and magic is in the air.*

December 19th and the email he'd been dreading, dropped
into his inbox. It was decorated with holly - naturally - and
unlike the standard communications from Global Standards
Inc, it was unusually cheerful. This alone was good reason to
be suspicious. It was just as he'd thought; confirmation of the
Christmas event with full directions to Holly Cottage. The
itinerary read like a game show, and they were all expected
to participate in that ridiculous Secret Santa game where one
had to purchase a gift for a colleague. His selected recipient
was highlighted at the bottom of the email. He glanced at
the name and rolled his eyes. Pauline Clayton had to be the
shortest straw going with regard to present buying. Despite
her being his personal assistant for more than two years, he
knew nothing about her. She was notoriously monosyllabic.
They hadn't even met, since all things administrative were
conduced by email or phone. And the limit was a tenner!
What was the point, exactly?

How would he survive this? Two nights trapped with
work colleagues he mostly despised or did his utmost to
avoid. It was one of those corporate events, but with none
of the perks of previous years so basically patronising and

embarrassing. Like lots of big companies, Global Standards Incorporated had thrown lavish Christmas parties in the old days. Dinner in a good London hotel, with a free bar for at least the first couple of hours and no pressure to represent the company with good behaviour. Those were the days! Gradually, the whole shebang had collapsed into not much more than a bottle of whisky and a pat on the back.

This year, some bright junior management spark - probably Dean Johnson - had excelled himself in the cost-cutting department. Johnson had already earned himself the title of Rudolph the brown-nosed reindeer and rumours were rife as to his expected promotion, the size of his bonus and just who he'd managed to pin down with his horn.

This year, the company had whittled Christmas down into a depressing blend of training and team-building; they'd even managed to slip in the yearly personal development interview on the afternoon they arrived. All of this was dressed up as a few days holiday with free paper hats; in several *self-catering* farmhouses across the UK. All the Global Standards Inc managers were fuming. Not only this, but the Wales and Greater Manchester division managers were booked into a remote Welsh cottage. A stupid idea in itself, travelling in December in a convoy of economy company cars along roads only fit for tractors. Snow, was in fact forecast for the week prior to Christmas and more than a handful of his colleagues prayed it would cause the entire expedition to be cancelled.

Sadly, it must have bypassed them because when it came around, December 19th was cloudy with sunny spells.

'You'd think a place called Snowdonia could manage a bit of snow for December, wouldn't you?' he said to Lynn.

'There's no point praying for snow *now*, be hell for travelling. They won't cancel it at this stage.'

'More like a punishment than any kind of reward, if you ask me.'

What was he meant to take? A business suit and a pair of walking boots? He pulled down his holdall and added denims and sweaters, one shirt and one tie, then rooted around in the bathroom cabinet.

'You'll be home before you know it,' Lynn said, arms crossed. 'There'll be alcohol, won't there?'

'Bloody hope so.'

'Should be fine, then.'

Rick kept his eyes on the mirror while he brushed his teeth. He could see her moving about their bedroom, picking up things and putting them down again. There were no decorations in the flat, nothing to suggest she'd planned Christmas or was even interested in the holiday. He didn't like to admit it, but he was disappointed. He knew it was maybe silly with no children between them, but he rather liked the idea of decorating a tree together over a bottle of wine and wrapping presents for each other. His Victorian flat lent itself to illusions of grandeur rather well, and he suddenly caught a vision in his mind's eye of his sitting room decked out in traditional reds and golds, the old floorboards sprinkled with glitter and the crackle of logs in the grate. There was plenty of room for a good-sized tree. He used to enjoy dressing the tree, even as a moody teenager, did a better job of it than his sister too. It was festive foreplay wasn't it? The build-up to the main event.

'What will you do for a couple of days without me? Hey, get a tree will you?'

Silence. 'Actually, Rick, I could do with talking to you about that.'

He wiped his mouth on a towel and added his toothbrush and shaving stuff to a wash-bag. He didn't like the sound of this. He didn't like the look of it either, her face was screwed up with a contrite expression, as if she were about to deliver bad news.

'There's no easy way to say this, but I'm moving out.

Sorry,' she said, flicking her eyes heavenwards, as if the whole thing was a drag.

'What… *now?'*

'Yeah, I'm *really* sorry but that girl I told you about? The photography studio in Tampa. Florida? Well, she's offered for me to go over for six months, there's some work in it, as well.'

'Great timing, Lynn!'

'It came out of the blue.'

She leant on the doorjamb with her arms crossed. 'Look, we're both grown-ups and we both know this isn't going anywhere. Well, don't we?'

Rick pushed past her and wondered what the hell to say. He was shocked, but he was perhaps more cross, mostly because she was right, so although he wasn't entirely surprised by her admission, the Christmas timing added an unwelcome barb to his dented pride. Not so much the icing on the cake but the secondhand greaseproof paper underneath.

He'd been living with Lynn for four months. He'd offered her a place to stay, and one thing had led to another. It was perhaps an admission of laziness on his behalf that the relationship was based on not much more than mutual sex and convenience. He hadn't fallen in love, but he thought he might have done. She was bright and funny, shared the same passion for city life and travel. It wasn't enough. Where was that elusive chemistry? He'd managed to avoid it most of his life. Maybe he was looking too hard; maybe he was looking in the wrong place, or standing in the wrong queue.

He threw his wash-bag into the holdall, and zipped it up. 'Okay, I can't lie, I knew you'd be off, sooner or later.'

'Really? That makes me sound horrible, like I've been using you. No, don't answer that,' she said, throwing up her hands. 'I *have* been using you, I've hated not paying my way.'

'You were in a bad situation.'

'I know, and I'll always be grateful, but I need to work and I *need* to pay you back.'

'Well, congratulations. You've paid me back in full. Christmas alone is only what I deserve.'

She looked at the floor and the ceiling, everywhere except at him. 'Don't be bitter, Rick. It was fun.'

'While it lasted? I'm not bitter,' he said. 'It's more pride. I wish you'd given me some warning.'

'I only got forty-eight hours to think about it. We're still friends? Please say we are.'

'I think maybe we should have *stayed* at friends, don't you?'

They had an awkward conversation about the rent, an awkward embrace, an awkward moment at the door saying goodbye and good luck. She'd be gone by the time he returned, a matter of days before Christmas. He barely had time to take in what was happening, all his mind registered was that it was going to be a miserable holiday. Could he possibly travel down to Cornwall and stay with his parents? Bloody hell, no. His sister would be there with the children. It would be all arguments and strained atmospheres. And Lynn was her friend so there'd be questions, questions.

Already late, he used it as an excuse to get away from her and took the lift. He nosed his car out of the underground car park and joined the slow-moving traffic. He almost took the motorway exit when he remembered the present for Pauline Clayton. Cursing, he went round the roundabout again - horns honking - and turned into the supermarket car park. The usual pathetic Father Christmas wearing a droopy red suit and rattling a bucket of coins stood close to the busy entrance, carols blaring from some awful sound system. Inside, it was packed full, a seething mass of shoppers dragging bawling children and pushing heavily laden trolleys full of junk food and cheap crackers. There were no wire baskets left but he only intended to pick up a box of chocolates and some fizzy wine but then on a whim, grabbed a bottle of Jack Daniels as well. Just in case.

The queues were nightmarish. A glance at his watch confirmed he was an hour later than he'd intended. He had no idea where Gwydyr Forest was and it grew dark so early, there was a high possibility of getting stranded in some godforsaken wilderness. He went back to the wines and spirits and grabbed a bottle of Remy Martin as well, just in case.

Someone tapped him on the shoulder. 'Is that all you've got? You're in the wrong queue.'

That figured. He allowed himself to be coerced towards the self-service tills, by a teenager wearing one of those microphones on a tinsel covered headset. Of course the bloody thing didn't work. He stood the bottles on the only available surface and the automated voice piped up. Yes, of *course* there were *unexpected items in the bloody bagging area*, there was nowhere else to put them while he hunted for his reading glasses! Several shoppers looked round, united in their hate of not only the system, but of the jobsworth staff in control of it, marching up and down the aisles issuing orders, channelling unsuspecting customers past the row of closed checkouts and into the jaws of public embarrassment; the electronic equivalent of those brown-nosed employees that never complained and made the job impossible for mere mortals. Who cared if they had oversensitive bagging areas? They worked unsociable hours for nothing more than a chip and when they were required to speak, the voice was always patient, controlled and modulated. Overall, they didn't answer back, never formed opinions and rarely went off sick.

It reminded him of Global Standards Inc. Too much fawning middle-management and the pretence that everyone was working as a happy team. It was thoroughly depressing and not for the first time he wondered if it was his age that made him so tired and cynical, or the fact that the season of goodwill tended to bring out the worst in people. The seething greedy mass of materialism rose to a frightening crescendo at this time of the year. Maybe it was the pressure to be happy? What he wouldn't give to feel that child-like joy at the sheer prospect of sharing Christmas with someone who simply desired his company.

He stowed his purchases in the boot, then went to get the Sat-Nav out of the glove compartment and everything fell out, including his present for Lynn. He'd bought her a crystal embellished watch. When he plucked it from it's satin bed and held it up, the dull December light still managed to make it sparkle. The whole world sparkled, when love was in the air, with or without the crystal embellishments. What had made him spend so much money? He knew he couldn't buy love - but he did have feelings for Lynn. Clearly, they were one-sided. Clearly, he'd misread the signals somewhere along the way.

He slung the box to the back of the glove compartment and tapped in the address of Holly Cottage, Gwydyr Forest. Drive time was only a couple of hours but it was already dusk and he hated looking for places in the dark, so he put his foot down. Slade came on the radio. How old was that track? He'd have been a teenager when that was charting. Why did people cling to this old, worn-out stuff like an unwashed, comfort blanket? Reliving their youth? He'd hate to relive his! He'd hate to start sounding like his parents as well.

'Music in our day was proper music.' This was his father's mantra. 'You could hear all the words, not like this modern rubbish.'

Interior decor aside, Rick liked modern stuff. Even at thirty-six he considered himself a lover of contemporary music and film, whatever was currently popular. All art had its origins in the past but things changed and moved on, developed and improved. He considered people who lived in the past to be small-minded and stuck in a rut. A lot of his friends still dressed like they did in the 90s. They looked like teenagers trapped in old bodies, like they were trying to prove something.

'I've still *got it*,' his dad would say. This was when he was dancing or singing, usually drunk. No, he couldn't go there, much as he loved his parents and sister, turning up single yet again meant being subjected to the same interrogations over and over.

'You know what your trouble is, don't you?' his sister had said the previous Christmas Eve, 'You're too uptight to let yourself fall in love.'

As he belted along the motorway his sister's words needled away. He couldn't remember the last time he'd told someone he loved them, but what was the point if they didn't feel the same? He wasn't given to emotional overtures at the best of times. His nickname in the office was Rick-the-Reserved for a damn good reason. He turned Slade off. Why had Lynn felt the need to escape so quickly? Should he text her, wish her a safe journey, wish her a happy Christmas on the beach, or what?

North Wales was cold and grey but at least he was relieved from the monotony of the motorway. A rough, narrow lane climbed, steep and twisting with no passing places for two miles and brought him to a hamlet consisting of a farm, an old public telephone box and a broken wooden bridge straddling a raging stream. Holly Cottage looked grim. There was a large area for parking to one side, and he recognised the row of blue cars, most of them with white tyres from all the loose stones filling the pot-holes on the access road. The Sat-Nav proclaimed he'd reached his destination. Rick climbed out and stretched.

Mostly fir trees, in every direction.

It smelt amazing, sharp and clean. It was a Christmas smell, like woodsmoke and spice. He'd never been one for the big outdoors but there was something about certain times of the year that made him yearn to fill his senses with something other than the stench of office politics. It looked as if there was a chance of this after all, but when he pushed open the wooden door, stooping to avoid banging his head, he was met with the usual discord when large groups of alpha males came together. A cluster of men arguing about how best to light the fire, and a handful of females organising the kitchen and pouring wine. All of this struck him as probably sexist, but he had to smile when the head of human resources, Helen Goulding, was the only one to get a flame going. So there was a use for that department after all. Fanning the embers of discontent had always been a speciality.

'Alderman! Fucking late as usual,' Len Dickson grumbled. His boss looked suitably naff in ill-fitting denims and a bright sweater. It made a change though, from his ill fitting suits and bright ties.

'Your personal development review should have been at four,' Dickson said.

'Traffic was terrible.'

'My *arse.*'

A quick consultation with the chart on the wall confirmed he was in room six, a single room on the second landing. Thank Christ for that, most of the rooms were twin-bedded. It was cramped, with a washbasin and a slanted window set into the roof. The bathroom was down the creaky landing, but at least there was full internet and telephone signals, which was unexpected. When he lay across the bed he could see the tops of the trees and the dank, grey sky. Where was Lynn now, already boarding the plane to sunnier climes? Maybe he should have made her wait till after Christmas, then suggested he went with her for a holiday? But Dickson wouldn't allow that, not at such short notice, and anyway, Lynn hadn't suggested it. She'd waited till he was backed into a corner with work commitments, then made her escape. He wondered about sending a text again but decided against it. Her mind was made up, so be it.

Dinner was a good distraction. He looked round the table and tried to work out which female was Pauline Clayton. He almost choked on his spaghetti when the blonde next to him patted his arm and proffered a limp hand, no rings.

'You must be Rick. I'm Pauline, it's so nice to meet you at last.'

'Oh, likewise. How did you, er…?'

'I've looked at your profile on the company site,' she said, filling his glass with red wine. 'You're six foot one with dark hair, blue eyes and… single. You like travel, city life, modern art and studied engineering to degree level. And now you audit engineering companies and you're the lead auditor for greenhouse gas emissions for Global Standards Inc. In fact, your job has taken you all over the world and you prefer red wines, to whites.' She clinked her glass against his. 'Me too.'

Not so monosyllabic in the flesh. The flesh was on show as well, lightly tanned and straining ever so slightly within the confines of a black cocktail dress. She must have been freezing, and it looked a little out of place in a stone cottage but he let her chatter on, all about her late husband who'd died three years ago and how she was finally coming out of her shell.

'I'm back on the relationship market. I mean, I'm only in my mid-thirties, so why shouldn't I?'

'Oh, good for you.'

There was an after-dinner presentation by Dean Johnson, The Call to Action. Predictably, there was a lot of sniggering amongst the more senior managers, which quickly turned to quiet outrage and disbelief when they realised that not only were they expected to audit their specific field of expertise, but they were also required to sell new certification packages to companies as well.

'We're not bloody salesmen!' Rick said.

Everyone was surprised by this outburst as he was usually notoriously quiet, and for good reason. No one would ever back him up when it came to putting his neck on the line, and bloody Rudolph was soon explaining how fifty-per-cent of the sales team had been made redundant and how lucky they all were to be still employed. Clearly, the upper echelons of management had seen fit to get this bombshell in at the start and out of the way.

'Well, I agree with Rick,' Pauline said, turning her grey eyes towards his. 'And it's going to be an administrative nightmare.'

'There'll be *training*,' Len Dickson said. Rather condescendingly, Rick thought.

'And there'll be the usual incentives,' Dean added.

'Wow. Training *and* incentives,' Rick said, mostly to himself.

Sounds of drunken discontent rumbled on, while Rick looked out of the corner of his eye at Pauline. She was quite classy, a bit keen to get acquainted but did he really care about that? She was probably only after some fun and companionship. She was likely lonely. Sex? Possibly. He filled her glass and smiled.

'I'm intrigued by your single status,' she said. 'Tell me to mind my own business, but you look like a family man to me.'

'Do I? How do you define that, exactly?'

'Solid, reliable, kind eyes.'

'Like a Labrador Retriever?'

She laughed huskily and leant in; musky perfume, slightly overpowering at close quarters. 'Yes, but without the roly bit in the middle.'

He was unsure whether to be flattered or not. She was certainly knocking the drinks back, but then so was he. This was the delicate dance of socialising with work colleagues, wasn't it? Although Pauline didn't carry the usual restrictions. The digital age meant they could behave as badly as they wished and never see each other again, whilst still maintaining a working relationship via email.

'So, why do they call you Rick-the-Reserved?'

'I think it's because I'm reserved.'

She laughed again and pushed his leg with hers. 'We'll have to see if we can change that. After all, it is Christmas.'

In the morning, when his watch alarm bleeped, his room seemed impossibly dark. He imagined this was down to the general lack of light and the December skyline crowded with trees, but when he finally turned on his back and glanced up, it was to see the Velux window full of snow. There was a pinprick of disturbance in the shape of a bird's foot, allowing a microscopic beam of light to filter down from a brilliant blue sky.

He checked his phone but there was nothing, no word from Lynn. She'd be flying though, wouldn't she? Up in the bright blue yonder; if flights hadn't been cancelled from Manchester. He was still unsure how he felt about Lynn upping and going with no warning, but when he turned over the bed was cold and he was suddenly, acutely aware of how much he missed her scent. She always wore something light and subtle, quite distinctive. It used to make him want to inhale more of it, to taste her skin. Sometimes he used to wake her by kissing her eye-lids.

He threw the duvet aside and made for the bathroom.

Downstairs, there was already some consternation about the depth of the snow and how on earth were they going to get all the cars safely back down the road? If you could call it a road! There were virtually no passing places and a sheer drop on one side. Rick wasn't concerned, after all, what did he have to rush home for? If they ran out of supplies there was a farm within walking distance and the village was only a two-mile walk back down the track. As he stood on the doorstep with a mug of coffee and inhaled the pleasantly pungent air he experienced faint stirrings of festivity. The fronds of the fir trees sagged with a good six inches of snow and the stream glinted like a dark glassy crevice, streaking through deep white folds. In the middle distance, just discernible through the forest were the taller peaks of Snowdonia, diamond sharp against a tanzanite sky. It looked like Narnia.

The itinerary was orienteering - in competing teams - followed by a motivational talk about planning work schedules and increasing customer-facing opportunities. This was titled Put-it-in-Your-Tool-Box, or some other such atrocious catchphrase. Then it was Christmas dinner, and Rick was on the rota to prepare vegetables. The mix of social and work-based themes made it difficult to feel motivated in any one direction.

When he was rooting about in the boot of his car for sensible footwear, Pauline materialised. Other than her pale face, she looked incredibly sleek and polished for a tramp through the snow. In daylight, he had to admit she looked astonishingly attractive. An expensive, dove grey ski jacket and the latest walking boots seemed as sexy as the black dress.

Lynn wasn't an outdoor girl. It wasn't as if she hated the countryside, neither of them did, they both preferred exploring historical ruins and art galleries if there was a choice. She'd have enjoyed the snowy forest though, in much the same spirit as himself. It seemed a shame that during the four months they'd been together, he hadn't got around to booking Rome; but then four months was the blink of an eye, wasn't it? Pauline caught his eye and wandered over.

'Isn't it beautiful? Like Disney.'

'Even Micky Mouse showed,' he said and inclined his head towards Dean Johnson and his boss, fussing with sheets of paper and a box of maps and compasses. She laughed, then moved in closer and tried to apologise for the previous evening.

'It was the first time I've let my hair down in... well, let's just say in a long while. I'd hate you to think I was cheap.'

'Of course I don't think you're cheap!'

He looked at the box of supermarket branded chocolates and the fizzy wine in his hands, and quickly shoved them back in the boot, out of sight.

'I mean, I'm sorry if I gave you the wrong impression. Oh dear, not making a very good job of this.'

He found his old boots and locked the car. 'Honestly, you didn't say anything untoward.'

'Oh, good. But I know I talked about myself, incessantly. Now, today it's your turn.'

'Not much good at that.'

Despite his standard protest, he found himself telling her about Lynn. He'd met her through his sister. She was married to a bully, and when this guy started hitting her, Rick offered her a room. He'd not really imagined she'd take him up on it, but she'd arrived one Sunday morning and that was that. Dark, petite, creative and butterfly-minded, she wasn't the sort of woman he was normally attracted to.

'I feel safe here,' she'd said. 'I like living on the second floor and I like the concierge on the desk.'

'Good.'

'Does it bother you, that Ian might come here and throw his weight around?'

'You mean, am I scared of a bloke who hits women? No.'

She didn't talk much about Ian but then he didn't really want to know the details. His sister listened to all that stuff. Then their relationship moved up a gear. Was sex inevitable? He was attracted to her in a quiet, slow-burn kind of way, with the feeling there was more to know. He didn't blame her for holding back after what she'd been through, but now he wondered if they should have talked more. Neither of them initiated a deep conversation. The first time they had sex it was just that, nothing more.

There was a dark bruise on her cheekbone which faded through the colour spectrum to a dull yellow, like saffron. The changes between them had been almost as subtle, moving from sessions on the sofa and the hearthrug, to more leisurely enjoyment in his bed. When he thought back to the last few weeks there was nothing - physically or emotionally - to suggest that it had been mere sex by that stage, it had definitely developed into *lovemaking*; which made her departure and her choice of words, deeply puzzling.

Aware that he'd been preoccupied, he glanced at Pauline. Although he'd not repeated these details out loud, she looked at him rather knowingly.

'Did you tell her how you feel?'

'I didn't get chance. I'm not even sure I know how I feel.'

'Too late now.'

'Some women. Complicated.'

'Some *men*. Reserved.'

He grinned.

'What are you doing for Christmas, then?' she said. 'You must have *some* plans.'

'Nothing. I'm hoping to get marooned here.'

'Head in the sand.'

'Look, what am I meant to do? Go chasing after her, all the way to Florida, possibly on a wild goose chase?'

'Depends. It might be a test.'

'And it might be the fact that she didn't like what she was getting into and decided to get out while she could. I don't play games.'

They walked across the car park, to where the main body of the group were standing around stamping their feet. Johnson was handing out sheets of paper. Cryptic clues and orienteering references, trees daubed with red or blue spots and numbers. Rick took one glance at his copy and passed it to Pauline.

Johnson clapped his hands. 'Okay, listen-up; to get the right answers you simply need to ask the right questions, just like getting all those sales leads we were talking about last night. If you don't ask the right question, you don't get the right answer. Think outside the box, yeah?'

There was some discreet groaning and foot shuffling. Pauline shot him a wry smile, while he more or less zoned out.

They were split into two groups and sent in opposite directions, competing against the clock. The rest of the Manchester crowd set off at a jog with himself and Pauline trailing behind.

'I hate this kind of thing,' he said.

'Even as a child?'

'Yep. Loathed games. I was the serious kid reading Lord of the Rings in the corner, while the rest of the boys ran about with footballs and started fights.'

'I find that perfectly possible to believe. Hey, we're getting left behind.'

'I refuse to run.'

They walked in companionable silence for some time, Pauline studying the clues and occasionally reading them out, but he couldn't equate how any of it would help him do his job more efficiently.

If you don't ask the right question, you don't get the right answer. What sort of reasoning was that? He'd never been any good at being forthright, which was why he did the job he elected to do and what he was employed for. He heard a burst of muffled laughter from the bowels of the forest. Maybe he was too serious. Maybe Lynn had found him too serious? Maybe he should have been more upfront and asked questions about their relationship and the *L word*. But then; would he have been prepared for the answer? And anyway, actions speak louder than words, don't they?

'Ten steps north...' Pauline was saying, compass in one hand, sheet of clues in the other, 'then take the left-hand track. Mr Poplar is very cross. Enter his office to discover your fate.'

Stooping beneath branches and scrambling over snowy rocks brought them to a clearing of poplar trees, dark and gloomy. One of the trees had a laminated sheet pinned to it with a red 45 in a circle. Pauline gave him a perplexed grin. 'What do you reckon?'

'P45?'

'Brilliant! So, now we track 45 degrees south in the *opposite* direction...'

His phone rang. It was his sister, Karen. 'Have you finished for Christmas yet?'

He explained where and what, and about the snow but she'd already heard all of his news, from Lynn.

'Have you heard from Lynn by any chance?' he said.

'Yes, but only a text. She's really excited about this job. Great opportunity for her.'

'Yeah, well. Bit unexpected, wasn't it? She might even be there by now. Is she... do you know?'

'She says it's lovely and warm for this time of the year. Beats all the crap weather in the UK.'

'Is that all she said?'

'More or less. Probably jet-lagged. Ah, well. I always thought, you two might... you know?'

'Did you?' He managed to laugh but it sounded hollow, even to himself. 'Not my type at all I'm afraid.'

'No, I did think that, actually. Never mind, are you coming over to Mum and Dad's?'

'Not sure yet. Not even done any present buying. Maybe New Year?'

He ended the call and looked across to Pauline. She was perched on an elevated bench overlooking a distant view, but in the quiet stillness he felt sure she must have heard his side of the conversation at the very least, if not all of it. The leaders of the group were now lost to sight, although occasional shouts could be heard echoing through the trees. He squinted at the sky and the harsh, cold sunlight bouncing off the virgin snow and fished about in his pocket for an old pair of shades.

His iPhone informed him where due south was and they headed down a track.

'I can't help feeling this is cheating,' Pauline said.

'It's called being sensible.'

'And we've only answered one of the questions on the sheet.'

'We've both been sacked according to Mr Poplar, so what's the point?'

She laughed. They were back at Holly Cottage in no time, but to a sea of angry faces. Manchester team had won by a couple of seconds but were then disqualified because two of the party hadn't participated. Rick found it tiresome. Dean Johnson was congratulated on devising and setting up the event in his own time, and the prize went to North Wales section.

The afternoon dragged on with a PowerPoint aided talk by one of the senior executives. Again, the slant was on front-line sales with a number of catchphrases blended into the spiel, presumably to add a 'fun' element. The speaker was over enthusiastic, like a time-share salesman.

'If, for example the client mentions that his strategic objectives for the next five years are to include a drive towards collaborative business relationships, you need, as an experienced auditor to collate this information for our sales hotline and...' he paused here to tap the side of his head, *'to put it in your toolbox.'*

Pauline had her head down, busily typing notes for Dickson. She was sitting next to old Booth, who looked as if he'd suffered a stroke. Booth nodded off in every single meeting in spectacular style, head lolling, slackened mouth, whereas Johnson was nodding in agreement for virtually every other sentence, oddly enough, with the same slack mouth.

The assumption that all of this was somehow new or clever, was thoroughly depressing. Was he in the wrong job? Lynn had had a lifetime of false starts, finally discovering her true vocation in commercial photography. Her eyes shone when she talked about the angle of light hitting the sides of buildings. She had a portfolio of such pictures, leaning skyscrapers with trees mirrored in them and herds of blurred commuters rushing past. He liked to look at the ones she'd taken around Italy and then there were dozens of close-ups, a study of grapes, vines and bottles for a vineyard. She had so much equipment, most of it, no doubt still in his second bedroom. And she was expressive and talkative. He hadn't seen much of this side of her personality but he knew it was there because it surfaced from time to time, then suddenly evaporated, retreated in the face of his reserve. And no doubt her bubble had been burst by that oaf she'd been married to and she'd put a veil of protection around herself.

Although he'd not said anything at the time he'd really felt for her, especially when he discovered she'd also lost her job through being off sick.

A voice cut into his thoughts. 'What do you think, Rick?'

'Sorry, what about?'

'Communications,' Johnson was saying. 'How can the company improve? Despite social networking, email, texting and telephoning we seem to have become a nation of poor communicators. You've been a classic example today. How shall I say… disengaged?'

'I don't know about anyone else but I've got an overload of information, so it needs more thinking time. Otherwise, I'm likely to spout waffle, and I can't see any of our clients being happy with that.'

There was a subtle intake of breath in the room, except for Pauline. 'And I think it's because we've given up on plain, simple talking,' she said quickly, and Rick applauded her. A couple of the others did too, and he met her grey eyes with a serious smile.

Rudolph, his nose cherry-red from his morning in the snow, scowled.

Later, Rick was called to action in the kitchen, preparing the vegetables. Pauline materialised in another stunning dress, silvery this time.

'You look fabulous,' he said, chopping carrots into batons.

'Thank you,' she said, and set about laying the table for fifteen.

Dinner was good, mostly because they could get to the alcohol again, although they were all warned that an on-line test-of-understanding needed to be completed in a timely fashion, before bedtime. Johnson passed the sprouts down the table and made some earth-shattering joke about Rick being the greenhouse-gas expert for Manchester section. All true, and having had time to reflect, Rick had to admit there was a grain of truth in Rudolph's earlier analysis. He *could* be disengaged, in fact that was probably how he came across most of the time, at least in his personal relationships because with business there were always facts and figures to stack up at the end of the day. How to measure love? Some people had no problem with it, and were both liberal and generous. He looked across to Helen Goulding, on her mobile yet again. 'Yes, yes, I love you too. Home soon. Love you, love you…'

'Oh, I *love* you too,' Rudolph said, and she snapped her phone off.

'Just because you haven't got a special someone.'

'No need to rub my nose in it, is there?'

A handful of people laughed, but the majority had

discreetly rolled their eyes at Helen. To Rick, the cheesy repetition watered it down to something worthless. When he said those three words to someone it would be a private affair, and certainly not shouted down a phone at the end of every blasted conversation.

Another speech followed, all about why there was no Christmas bonus but weren't all the managers lucky to have this wonderful meal together? Then it was presents and Secret Santa. Dean Johnson received a vibrator but no one was admitting to sending it. Rick saw him drop it into Pauline's handbag.

'What?' he said, spotting Rick's narrowed eyes. 'It's a massage wand. What do I want with that?'

'A magic wand, you say?' Pauline responded, and Johnson had the decency to look away. There was more to Pauline than he'd assumed. Not only did she have good taste, but she could hold her own with Rudolph.

Outside, the snow was already melting, making a slippery translucent mush of the car park. He couldn't give her those chocolates with less than seventy percent cocoa solids and the bottle of plonk containing only ten percent alcohol; he just couldn't. They were gifts for an older teenager, not a mature woman. It was insulting, especially given the way she'd stuck her neck out for him, listened to his moaning about the job and the complexities of his affairs of the heart. He slumped in the passenger seat and tried calling Lynn, then suddenly remembered Florida was eight hours ahead or something and she'd possibly be asleep, and so ended the call after one ring. He sighed and opened the glove compartment. The watch didn't need wrapping, the box was glamorous enough. He wrote her name on the gift tag and grabbing the bottle of cognac, made his way back across the slush.

All eyes swivelled his way when he placed the box down next to Pauline's mince pie, then retook his seat opposite.

She shot him a bemused look and carefully lifted the lid. She smiled; her expression gradually morphing into shock when she realised that the watch was real, and not borne of a cracker.

'This was more than ten pounds.'

'I'll say it was,' his boss said, leering over Pauline's shoulder. 'You need a salary cut if you can afford to give stuff like that to your P.A., eh Rick?'

'Just accept it as thanks for all your hard work over the past couple of years.'

'Well… I don't know what to say! Thank you seems so inadequate. And I've only bought you a bottle of shiraz and some salted caramels.'

'Lovely.'

There was a good fire going again, and this lent a more relaxed ambience over the coffee course. Leaving the debris on the table, everyone pulled chairs around the cavernous inglenook, except for Rudolph and a couple of the others who wanted to do the on-line test of understanding. The watch looked at home on Pauline's wrist, and she thanked him again, twisting it this way and that in the flickering firelight. They discovered that the salted caramels went rather well with the cognac.

'I'd like to ask you something,' she said. 'And please say no if I'm getting ahead of myself, but would you like to come for Christmas lunch?'

'Oh, well, I wasn't expecting that.'

'I overheard your conversation this morning and you sounded so low. I'm guessing you might be alone, for the big day?'

'Can I let you know?'

'Of course.'

Of course he hadn't been expecting that, but neither had she expected a Dolce & Gabbana watch from not-so-secret-Santa. She wasn't stupid, she'd likely also guessed that the watch had been purchased with someone else in mind. Had he messed-up already? Had she read more into it than he'd wanted to imply? But then she'd only invited him for a meal, she was good company and where was the harm? Above all, he'd hate to hurt her feelings.

'Actually, Pauline, I'd like to very much.'

She laughed. 'That didn't take much thinking about.'

'I guess you asked the right question.'

'Well, I certainly got the right answer.'

As a test of understanding, it gave him much the same kind of headache as the on-line version. Later, in his room, he took one glance at the email and almost logged off, then stabbed his finger on answer 'A' for every single question and to hell with it. Expecting staff to fill out a test when they were all borderline drunk, what sort of crass timing was that?

He grinned to himself as he stood under the shower; give Johnson something to do, sorting out the big mess of misunderstanding in the morning. Maybe he should have sent an email to Lynn too, but he was too drunk and likely to say the wrong thing.

A: Christmas together with a tree and presents. B: Christmas apart with no tree and no presents. C: Christmas with Pauline.

He'd have said option A, or something stupid like that. The only option which, in reality, was not on offer.

No surprise that virtually everyone failed the test of understanding. At breakfast, there was a blanket of silence, punctuated by the fizz of tablets in water and Booth grumbling about his peptic ulcer. Inside and outside reflected the general mood; grey, dripping and dismal. In the kitchen the aftermath of the previous evening looked especially depressing with a dripping tap and a pile of unwashed pots and pans. Outside, there was a slow thaw but more snow was forecast and Dickson made the decision to cancel the final training session called *Break the Mould - Let's Look at it Another Way*; in order for everyone to get home before dusk. There was a collective sigh of relief.

Everything was packed up in record time and a succession of tyres spinning on the gravelled slush, added to the general feeling of haste. Rick was summoned to his yearly assessment. Len Dickson looked bleary, but found enough bloody-mindedness to see it through. They covered the usual ground.

'How do you see yourself improving in the next year?' his boss said, shuffling paper. 'Well?'

This always stumped Rick. His track record was second to none; he was always meticulous and conscientious, and he usually hit targets. Whatever he said now would only serve his targets to be increased to a level slightly beyond feasibility.

'Feedback from clients is that you don't say much,' Dickson said, frowning at his laptop. 'Same as last year. So there's room for improvement there, wouldn't you say? Try to be more sociable, you know, make them feel valued by the company.'

'Valued by the company? I see.'

'And you've been pipped to the post this year with overall points. Dean Johnson has gone the extra mile and completed eight more client-facing days than you over the previous twelve months, and he's already pulling in sales leads. He always delivers does Dean.'

'Father Christmas must be proud. He'll be head reindeer in no time.'

'You could learn a thing or two from Johnson, you know.'

'Like, how to use up my holidays for work instead? Doesn't that contravene the work-life balance you keep banging on about?'

'He simply manages his time efficiently, that's all,' Dickson said, packing stuff into his briefcase. 'And he never asks a *closed* question, that's key in getting those sales leads.'

A closed question; the opportunity to answer *no, no thanks;* thus committing the conversation to a dead-end before it even started, before a foot could get in the door and draw out the truth. Should he have asked a more open question of Lynn? Something like… is this what you really want, or should we have a talk about our feelings before you go, because there's things I'd like to say? His thinking surprised him, travelling as it had along lines of reflection, and regret.

Outside, one finger in his ear, he tried her mobile again. She picked up after two rings and his heart actually raced.

'Lynn!'

'Oh! Rick…'

'How's it going?'

'Oh, you know…'

'Work huh?' he said, and faked a laugh. 'It must be hot in Florida.'

'It's like a British summer.'

'That can't be right, Christmas in the sun.'

'I never realised you were such a traditionalist.'

'Oh yeah, I love all that. We never really, you know… talked about Christmas, did we?'

'Too late now. What will you do?'

'Oh, you know. This and that.'

'Okay, well… I'll talk to you soon. Got stuff to do here.'

'Me too.'

He spotted Pauline making her way across the car park, dragging a suitcase on wheels with a pair of boots balanced on top. He was forced to say a hasty farewell to Lynn, then forced to smile at Pauline. She was holding the massage wand and pretending to draw letters in the sky. He was unsure how this made him feel. Any red-blooded man would be champing at the bit, but his overriding feeling was one of disappointment.

'You'll need my home address,' she said brightly. 'This magic wand might be clever, but it doesn't perform spells. Imagine the fun if it did?'

'You can... email me. Don't forget the post-code, for the Sat-Nav.'

'I won't,' she said, and moved in for a hug. It felt awkward because it was intimate even through winter coats. Or maybe it just seemed that way because of Lynn. He helped Pauline load the case into her car and then he was distracted by members of staff shaking hands, clasping each other in gestures of solidarity, full of Christmas bonhomie. A couple of them gave Rick a nod and a wink. So, everyone had noticed.

Driving back along Welsh roads, through hamlets he hadn't noticed on the way in, he was struck by all the homemade decorations in front windows, the plastic Santa clinging to the chimney and the tinsel trim on the farm gate. Holly and mistletoe for sale. The village chapel displayed a poster about its forthcoming Christingle service, bringing a rush of childhood memories. Oranges, impaled with candles. Light, warmth and love. That's what it was all about, wasn't it?

In contrast, the motorway journey was dark, cold and devoid of emotion. In accordance with this, the blue sign for Manchester International airport was dripping with dirty snow, but there seemed less of a thaw towards the city. He tried not to think of that as some kind of prophecy. He was undecided if it was a whim, or he'd been planning it all along, but he took the exit to terminal two without decreasing his speed. Parking was protracted and expensive. Intent on his destination, he didn't notice the flight information flashing on every available screen. When he approached the relevant airline desk there was no one checking in - because the runway was full of ice. He'd failed to notice the milling clusters of disgruntled passengers. Some of them were arguing with staff, some of them were sitting on cases and simply looked tired. He knew how they felt. No doubt some of them were facing a postponed holiday in the sun, but there would be others with no way of reaching loved ones for Christmas.

For Rick, it was unfinished business. It was the sort of business that couldn't be quantified and signed off, partially because he didn't actually want to finish it. He no longer needed to examine his feelings and pick over what this meant. It was just a shame it had taken so long to reach some kind of conclusion. Here he was, ready to make a dramatic, romantic gesture of epic proportion, with no way of implementing it. Maybe it would never have worked though, because on landing, he would have needed to contact her, to find out her exact address and the surprise would be lost. He had a vague idea, that was all.

He walked back through the concourse, wearing his shroud of misery like a cloak. There was a towering Christmas tree at the entrance, which he hadn't even noticed on the way in, and he stopped to look more closely. A modern conical vision of reds, purples and pinks pulsing with lights. Around the base there was a deep drift of polystyrene chips and what he could only describe as a continental nativity scene - the Three Kings were respectively black, white and yellow. To one side there was a nodding donkey with a collection box chained to one of its hind legs. A security camera watched over the scene like the star of Bethlehem.

It was hideous.

His feelings for Lynn went far deeper than he'd cared to admit three days ago. He already missed her, bitterly. The thought of his apartment, cold and empty, filled him with dread. *Lynn*. He simply longed to know more. And now the bloody woman had gone! Maybe it was for the best, she hadn't exactly encouraged any commitment from him let alone invited him over as a last minute gesture. Outside the brightly lit airport building, it was fully dark. The first flakes of snow began to settle on the windscreen as he drove home. The streets were busy, greasy with new snow touching old slush. He didn't even stop for groceries, comforting himself with the idea of walking to the pub later and eating there. Or maybe just drinking.

The other thought which struck him was that of hooking up with Pauline. It would only go to cement what he'd known all along; his P.A. would be second best, second choice. No, it was no good, he'd have to cancel her, better to hurt her feelings now than get into something he'd regret after they'd slept together. Or, worse than that, shared a false Christmas. Rick the Reserved would have to brace himself and speak out. *Break the mould.*

She answered immediately. 'Hello! I was just thinking about you.'

'Oh?'

'I've got something to tell you.'

'Me too, listen Pauline I-'

'Can I speak first? I think I know what you're going to say. I'm not a mind-reader but I know when someone is besotted with love, consumed by it.'

This was awful. What on earth did he say to this? 'I don't know what to say,' he mumbled, embarrassed. Could she have fallen in love with him that quickly?

'I do,' Pauline said. 'Go and find her!'

'Oh, you mean Lynn? She's thousands of miles away.'

A huge sigh, then a laugh. 'Rick. Have a wonderful Christmas… *somehow.*'

It was quite the strangest conversation, but thankfully with no particular distress. There was however, another lightbulb moment of sorts. Not a 100 watt blinding flash, more of a slow illumination, like soft romantic candlelight. It was just himself then, who couldn't see it.

He clambered out of his car and opened the boot to

remove his holdall. He clamped the box of chocolates under his free arm and grabbed the bottle of wine. It was perfectly chilled. The lift trundled to the second floor and he walked along the corridor deep in thought. At his front door, he was nonplussed to see a wreath pinned there, full of tartan bows and twinkly lights. When he pushed the door open, his senses were engulfed with the scents of warm pastry and spice, like cinnamon. Slade was blasting out and someone, somewhere inside his apartment, was singing along to it. His first thought was that he'd been invaded by squatters. He dropped the holdall and ventured carefully into his sitting room expecting to see a row of sleeping bags and a camp, but the room was like the centre-spread of Ideal-Home magazine.

At first he was fully captivated by the tree; a real specimen, scraping the ceiling and festooned with tartan bows, wooden decorations and white lights. Beneath the lower branches there were presents in a haphazard pile. On the fireplace, there was a basket of fresh-cut logs and a circle of fat church candles. Next to this, more fairy lights entwined through tall branches of willow standing ram-rod straight in his one and only vase. There were cards and someone had arranged them artfully on the wall, like a collage.

He walked through to the kitchen and there she was, lifting a tray of mince pies out of the oven. His kitchen was a mess; in fact he couldn't recall ever using the cake tin or the measuring spoons, but it filled his heart with an effervescence like bubbles of champagne. He switched off the radio and she spun round, swiping at her fringe with a floury hand. Her face freeze-framed with bemused shock, and he felt sure his own face took a few seconds to become animated.

'Lynn!'

'I can explain,' she said, then looked at the wine and the chocolates, still crushed under his arm. 'Are those for me?'

'Not really, but you can have them if you want. They're a bit cheap and nasty.'

She took them with a grin, and he rubbed his eyes in case she was an apparition. When he dared to look through his fingers, she was still there.

'I've just been to the airport,' he said slowly, with deliberately weighted words.

She smiled a delicious smile which lit up her eyes, and she licked the cake mixture off a wooden spoon. 'Why?'

'*Why?* To see if I could get a flight out to Florida!'

'I didn't go.'

'Clearly not. But you *said* you had. First to my sister and then when I called you… why did you lie?'

'I didn't lie! You never actually asked me. We just talked about the weather, everyone knows it's sunny in Florida. You don't have to be there to know that.'

'Good grief. So why *didn't* you go, what about the job? Did that not exist either?'

'Oh yes, it did,' she said, and dropped the spoon into the washing up, then folded her arms. There was a touch of defiance about her body language, but her eyes and her voice, were considerably softer. 'I wanted to stay here, with you. And curl up by the fire, and just… talk.'

'Talk?'

'And maybe, kiss?'

'Kiss?'

'Are you going to repeat everything I say, or are you going to think up your own words?'

'I love you.'

Jim's Christmas Carol

Santa and Satan pay a visit. One brings presents,
the other an unwelcome presence.

Jim

The trouble with extra-marital affairs is that when it comes to big family occasions like Christmas, there's always a hullabaloo. Carol knew he was married of course, but that didn't stop her moaning that she'd be all alone on the big day, and this was despite the fact that she'd been invited to several parties and festive occasions, so hardly alone. She always liked to remind him of his absence at pertinent times of the year, and she'd taken to wearing a pair of dangerous dangly earrings. They looked like serpents and practically poked his eye out when they were in bed together.

Not only this, they were tacky. If he was honest, her entire house was tacky; decorated in that awful wood-chip paper from the seventies and then painted in dark colours. It was hopelessly untidy too with an old piano, stacks of books and drooping spider plants - and this was in the bedroom. It was like a student bedsit on a grand scale, but it was an amazing aphrodisiac. His wife liked classic, clean lines with paint shades from Farrow and Ball, and there were no houseplants because of the mess they made. In theory, he tended to agree with Kath, but at Carol's house he was allowed to be a sex-beast-slob, and she never produced a list of DIY jobs. Carol had no interest in housework, cooking or cleaning. In truth, he was unsure what she did for a lot of the time. He was aware of her loose reputation but it was mostly unfounded, she simply believed in the expression of free love, like a new-age hippy. She charged for reading Tarot cards, and frequently read his palm, although he tried to steer clear of that sort of thing and always laughed when she said the High Priestess was on his tail. In truth, he thought her quite vulnerable behind this silly facade she liked to cultivate. She wasn't quite so self-sufficient in the emotional stakes as she liked everyone to think, and she'd become increasingly more demanding of late.

Christmas Eve. He'd managed to get away on the pretext of a spot of mystery shopping, and to collect their son from the train station.

Carol straddled his white body. She had no inhibitions, her physical form was a vessel for his pleasure and she easily brought him back to life with her younger, more vigorous enthusiasm. Ironically, he could hear a brass band in the shopping precinct plodding through a repertoire of carols. After a particularly rousing version of O-Come-All-Ye-Faithful; one of the silver serpents went missing. She was distracted then, searching the bed and the floor. Jim was pleased, maybe she'd remove the other one now, but she claimed they were a symbol of power and did her bidding, or something equally ridiculous.

After a short while, she gave up. It was bitterly cold; but she stood naked at the window, lighting a small cigar with a disposable lighter. Thankfully, there was a swathe of purple net curtain - it smelt of old dust - between her and any passersby in the street. Not that it would have bothered her if someone had stopped to take a closer look; she'd been into nudist colonies and dipping her breasts in mud at pop festivals all her life. This was all very well but her house overlooked the train station and sometimes, droves of people would emerge and automatically look up at the house with its brace of ugly gargoyles staring down from the roof. On this occasion, his son was due to arrive on platform one from Cardiff, but there was at least twenty minutes. Plenty of time.

'What's happening then, on Christmas Day?' she said. 'Will I get to see you?'

'Oh, you know, the usual. The High Priestess will knock herself out making a Christmas to remember. I'll be sucked in, hanging sparkly balls and laying the fire, decanting the port.'

She wandered across to the bed and said something crude about balls, his big ship sailing into port and setting it on fire. He was always bemused, sometimes shocked by her behaviour and some of the things she said, but he was addicted to the sleaziness of it. The whole package took him back to his youth. He'd tried to stop seeing her once before, but failed dismally. His other failure was that he felt increasingly uncomfortable talking about Kath with any kind of derision. His wife had done nothing to deserve his scorn other than be preoccupied with making a home to be proud of. Since Adam had left for university she'd started to take some time out. He wondered if she might return to work, but at forty-five and living where they did, what on earth would she do? Instead, she'd joined the local drama group and taken to pottery classes. He didn't begrudge any of this - she'd brought up their son single-handedly. 'I can't get out of family commitments, nor do I especially *want* to,' he said gently. 'I'm looking forward to seeing Adam.'

'So you keep saying.'

'Do I? Look, you knew what the score was when we first got together.'

'We're not together.'

'You know what I mean. I told you I was married that first afternoon.'

'You imagine because you've *told* me about your family you are now exempt from any guilt, is that it?'

He sighed and began to hunt for this clothes. Not this again. Perhaps he shouldn't have expressed his feelings aloud. It did sound patronising, as if he was accusing her of stopping him being a father, or merely using her for sex. But then, he was, wasn't he? He needed to be careful, he couldn't imagine life without his delicious cake. Kath didn't even offer crumbs these days, let alone let him eat it. She rubbed his nose in his dirt at every opportunity, and he'd not get a second chance.

Carol crossed to her card table and shuffled her pack of Tarot cards, then began to lay them out with careful consideration. She sat with her legs apart, deep breathing, dark hair falling forward and hiding her face. If there was a single most irritating aspect of her company, it was this obsession with the Tarot. She was striking to look at, slim with strong features and incredible breasts, where Kath was fair and slightly plump. He kept hinting at taking some exercise but she always maintained looking after their spacious house and the garden was more than enough.

Since Carol was closed off from him during this ritual with the cards, he switched on the ancient shower down the hall. The sight of his paunch and his bald spot had him think twice about some of the remarks he'd made to Kath. He soaped vigorously, under the intermittent jets of water for as long as he could stand it, then made his way back to the bedroom shivering; a dark-green, equally balding towel around his waist and a greyish white one across his shoulders. Carol was still hunched over her felt-topped table, like some medieval witch.

'Go on, what am I today, The Hanged Man? Or The Fool?'

'The Hermit. It's presenting alongside the Four of Cups, so not as obvious as you might think. It makes a difference to how the major Arcana is interpreted.'

'Rubbish.'

'Tell me, what do you believe in, exactly?'

'Well not that mumbo-jumbo for a start,' he said, rubbing the towel briskly across his back. 'I see nothing to set apart those pretty cards of yours from say, the bible, or the horoscopes in the Sunday paper. They all play on weakness.'

'You must be a *very* strong man. Are you an atheist?'

'Yep. And that means I'm in charge of my own destiny,' he said, trying to get socks over his damp feet and hopping into the dusty furniture. 'Ouch!'

She sighed and flicked another card onto the table. 'Christmas must be a strain for you. All that worshipping to get through.'

'It's about *family*, and having a rest from work.'

She flinched slightly and he immediately regretted the choice of words but what the hell, wasn't that the truth? He was about to say something to soften the blow when she turned the final card, and he heard her intake of breath. He began to fashion a knot in his tie and glanced over her shoulder. *Death.*

He laughed. 'Going to drop dead, am I?'

'I'm telling you, this is a bad combination.'

'Poppycock. All of it, utter tosh.'

He sensed her deep disapproval but couldn't risk any further discussion on the subject as he needed to be out of the house before Adam's train pulled in. He dived down the stairs, already loosening his collar slightly and smoothing his hair. He hesitated on the step, hand poised to pull the door shut. The noise and vibration of the trains rumbling into the station, and the incomprehensible babble of the announcements somehow served to galvanise his thoughts. *Damn it.* He needed to finish this. The two-week Christmas break would be perfect timing, no awkwardness catching the train for a while, give her chance to get used to it. He pushed the door open again and shouted up the stairs, glancing anxiously at his watch. She appeared on the landing, calm but resigned.

'Don't even think of finishing this again, or you'll live to regret it. I won't be used and messed about.'

Heart pumping, he advanced part-way back up the stairs to plead his case. There was a hideous stuffed crow suspended from the light fitting, and he knew it was there but this time for some unfathomable reason, he walked straight into it and had to bat it away.

'Carol, wait! Let's take a break, then? Just over Christmas, please? Come on, you said you had invitations… choices.'

Looking down from her elevated position on the landing, there was something menacing about the way she held those nicotine stained cards over her chest. Even the bloody crow, swinging round in a circle had him ducking out of its way again.

'Don't even think about it,' she snarled.

He rubbed ineffectively at the dent on his forehead, courtesy of one dead beak. 'Look, we'll talk after Christmas… I have to go, I'll be late for Adam.'

He backed out, knowing he wasn't released, even when he'd pulled the door shut, he could feel a weight bearing down on him. Well! That hadn't been on the cards a few minutes ago. So much for thinking he was in charge of his own destiny.

Adam

Maybe she imagined no one could see her behind that flimsy curtain, but when the sun was sinking behind the house, her naked form was perfectly visible. Like those silhouettes of dancing women at the beginning of a Bond film. They always repeated them at Christmas, didn't they? He watched that stuff with his dad. Christmas at home doing naff things with your parents was one of the essentials, wasn't it? It meant you got to moan about it to your mates whilst secretly enjoying it and posting random pictures of your mate's sister's starter bra on Facebook. The Cardiff train was early so he loitered on the station steps, hoping to catch an eyeful from the house of ill repute across the road, and wondering whether to text his dad. Then a few minutes later, something happened that he wished he could erase from his memory. The door opened, and his dad came out. He seemed preoccupied for a few seconds, then marched back inside and left the door swinging. Had he just imagined that? What the hell was his dad doing in there?

As he crossed the street, avoiding the build-up of brown slush, a fresh swirl of snow blurred his vision. He hesitated on the pavement, his eyes fixed on a hoarding advertising a Christmas pantomime and some local church concert. He heard raised voices, indistinguishable words; but their meaning was clear. When his father reappeared he was agitated. Their eyes met and in that second of recognition, he managed to change his thunderous expression to one of shocked surprise, as if he might burst out laughing any second.

'Adam!'

'What were you doing in there?'

He closed the door fully behind him and whisked an arm across his shoulders, taking his bag and propelling him towards the station car park. He cleared the snow from the windscreen and rubbed his hands together with an expression of pretend excitement. How old did he think he was, six? Then he started the engine and whacked the heater full-on. After a while, he began to ask the usual questions about Uni.

Adam stared through the passenger window. They headed out of town, along increasingly snowy roads towards Rowen. Their house was on the outskirts of the village along a single-track road bordered by the huge ancient trees of a wood. Although it was private land, he'd played in there as a kid or collected kindling for the wood-burner. Sometimes, he'd just watched the birds or the insects. In the other direction there was normally far-reaching views across the hills but the snow was obliterating everything beyond a few metres like cold, grey smoke. The house was impressive, full of tasteful decorations and twinkling greenery. When he'd been at primary school his friends used to think he lived in a mansion and they always wanted to come for stop-overs and set up camp in the woods. Then through secondary school it somehow became a huge embarrassment having a house bigger than everyone else, and it was miles from anywhere he wanted to be. He'd worked like a dog in Funky Chicken to get the deposit together for a car, but now it mostly stood idle because it cost a fortune to run, and anyway, there was nowhere to leave it at Uni.

Now though, when they rounded the bend in the road and the house came into view, he felt a surge of pride and contentment. Maybe it was the fact he'd been away since the middle of September and it looked so different. Or, maybe it was because *he* was different?

'You're quiet, you must have *some* news,' his dad said.

'What were you doing in that house?'

He chuckled and started rifling through his coat pockets, something he did when he was nervous. He pulled out a handful of sweet wrappers and an old cloakroom ticket. 'Keep it to yourself, but I was having my cards read. Tarot cards?'

'You hate that sort of thing.'

'I know, but I drew the short straw in the office tombola,' he said, unfolding the cloakroom ticket for verification. 'Just a bit of fun, but you have to go along with this stuff otherwise they all think you're a spoilsport.'

Adam wasn't sure what to think about this. The Chester office was notoriously stuffy, he couldn't imagine them having a tombola drum with members of staff picking out random prizes. *Oh, what fun! I got a prostitute voucher, thank you very much Mr Watson-Brown, how terribly kind of you.* Yeah… *right.*

Once inside, he tipped-up his bag in the utility room, no point unpacking it, really. His mum threw the usual set of questions at him, scolding him for being so untidy, then nagged his dad to set the fire. 'Oh, *Jim*… there's bird-dirt all down the back of your coat, did you know?'

He escaped to his room with a handful of mince pies and no plate. He kicked his bedroom door open and flung himself across the bed. His room looked childish. It was true, about being away from home, even just for a short time it made you think about stuff. Not that he'd ever admit that to his parents, and certainly not to his dad. They'd had some humdinger arguments about religion and vegetarianism. He'd met this girl at Uni; called herself Luna. She was into the natural forces of nature, especially the cycle of the moon. Somehow, she made sense of all those weird feelings he'd had since he was small and playing in the woods. If he'd known it had a name, then he'd have felt so much better about it. Now, he could say he was into Wiccan culture. A lot of the other students laughed, and he had to admit, it was all a bit seventies and confused with witchcraft but he liked the simplicity of it; whereas straight Christianity needed a much bigger leap of faith to comprehend what was virtually a fairy story. The law of threefold return was especially interesting in that any deed - good or evil - was returned back to the doer, threefold.

Do what you will, so long as it harms none.

Later, downstairs in the kitchen, his dad was already hitting the Christmas booze and reading the paper, while his mum was chopping and slicing. His dad's coat swung on a wire coat hanger in the utility room. It looked like a hanged man, a damp section across the back where it had been scrubbed between the shoulder blades. He wandered through to the sitting room first, pausing at the nativity scene they'd had since he was a child. There was a safe coziness about it. The Christmas tree, bedecked in artificial finery had pride of place in the window. That was rooted in paganism, wasn't it? What an eclectic mix of rituals. None of it made much sense when you threw it all together. Still, if it did no harm, he was cool with that.

Back in the kitchen, his dad poured him a beer.

'Adam! Come on, take a pew and tell us your news. How's the History going?'

He pulled out a chair at the massive limed-oak table and flipped his iPad open. 'Okay.'

His dad was pissed already, he had that look about his eyes, shaking out the paper and talking loudly. 'Can you *not* elucidate on that?'

'How was the train journey, Adam?' Mum said.

'Okay. Early.'

'Oh? That makes a change! Did you have to wait around in the cold?'

'Not really. Dad was already there, having his cards read over the road.'

'In the shopping centre?' his mum said, automatically.

He averted his eyes. His mum thought they were talking about Christmas cards at first, then gradually got drawn in. More uncomfortable laughter and the same story about tombola. His mum swallowed it, but she wasn't aware of the full story, the naked whore at the window, the way he'd come out of the house then gone back in. The angry words, his face and his *chortling*. Then his mum was distracted, irritated with their papers, phones and iPads and began to pile plates and cutlery on the side of the table. 'What cards did you get?'

'Oh, I can't remember, didn't take much notice.'

Adam caught his eye. 'You must be able to remember something, it was only a couple of hours ago.'

He lowered his paper, a tad crossly. 'Alright, but don't get alarmed by it. It's just a bit of fun and it doesn't mean anything. It was Death, the Four-of-Cups and The Hermit, I think, something like that. Now, I don't want to hear any more about it.'

His mum served a platter of stir-fry, shunting a chicken-free version across to himself. He was starving and helped himself to a big spoonful of brown rice, but not before he'd searched Death, The Hermit and the Four-of-Cups via Google, and bookmarked the pages.

Nell

It was an awful journey for a lone woman in her seventies, what had she been thinking? The snow started to come in as she reached the North Wales border and the distant mountains were like granite and mist, a blur one moment, a sketchy outline the next. Traffic slowed to a crawl, wipers full-on. She should never have agreed to drive herself all this way. Windermere to the Conwy Valley in bad weather, madness! But then, last Christmas had been awful too, her first alone since Graham's funeral. She'd wanted to shut herself away, wallow in her grief and cry when she felt like it, without family and friends - as well-meaning as they were - offering endless tea and sympathy. Christmas had been something to get through, not enjoy. This year, she wanted it to be different. Her daughter's home was so welcoming and she was ready to be taken back into the family fold. She no longer collapsed into a blubbery mess at random moments, she was ready to face the world again.

Kath had bought her a mobile phone. It had taken weeks to get the hang of it but she'd been determined, and now, as she turned towards Rowen in the increasing snow, she was eternally grateful for its presence in her handbag. It was the steep driveway she dreaded, but to her relief, Jim must have been out with a shovel and some gravel as it was mostly clear and she awarded herself a moment of congratulation as she finally parked next to her grandson's Mini. She took a moment to admire the outside lights, like shoals of fallen stars caught in the conifers and the ornamental shrubs. Even though it was still only Christmas Eve afternoon, the light was subdued enough to render the scenery magical.

'I made it, Graham,' she said, then eased herself out of the warm car.

The house was part Elizabethan, with leaded, mullion windows to the front. There was a wreath on the front door. Fronds of blue spruce twisted into a circle with red baubles, and a red bow across the top. She baulked slightly at this, reminding herself it had nothing to do with funerals, it was merely a traditional decoration and wasn't the circle of evergreen meant to symbolise strength? She needed some of that. Before she could knock, the door opened wide and her daughter was there, her eyes already filling, an arm across her shoulders, a hand grabbing her small holdall and the hastily wrapped Christmas cake.

Kath shouted in the direction of the stairs. 'Adam! Get the rest of Gran's bags from the car will you, please?'

'There's no rush,' she said.

Kath ushered her through to the sitting room, then went to make tea.

There was a wonderful fire crackling in the hearth - Jim was good at making a blaze. There was nothing to equal the heat and comfort from a real fire - and Nell warmed her hands gratefully and admired the room. Her daughter had all the right touches when it came to making a home, walls and floors a restful palette of creams through to buttery yellows. There was a comfortable mismatch of dark furniture and tapestry sofas with an abundance of books, squashy cushions and throws. And of course, taking pride of place, the tree! The old glass baubles she and Graham had bought in Austria were perfect.

'Oh, Kath, it looks wonderful,' she shouted through to the kitchen.

There was a happy mumble and a rattle of crockery in response, and Nell began to remove her coat and scarf.

On the hearth, there were candles in Victorian hurricane lamps and the ceramic snowman they'd bought together at an antique fair in the summer. Her eye caught something silvery, suspended by a thread on the woodpile and at first she thought it was something off the tree, but when she went to retrieve it, saw that it was an earring, a silver snake with a red eye. Not knowing where to place such a delicate thing, she popped it in her pocket for safekeeping. It wasn't the sort of thing Kath would wear, but then she was distracted by a black and white photo of herself and Graham. It had been taken on their wedding day, and the nostalgia was heightened somehow by the flickering tea-lights. She lifted the heavy frame and studied it carefully. *Fifty* years ago; they'd been not much older than Adam. How they'd loved and laughed! All those years… and now he was gone from her.

A couple of months previous, on Graham's birthday, she'd felt especially desperate. They'd been planning to take a cruise, planned it for years in fact, but instead of sailing into the sun, she'd had to bury him. Her grief reached a crisis point. Too distracted and confused to cry, she'd climbed into the car. Graham had insisted she learnt to drive in her fifties - no mean feat - but he'd been so patient. If she didn't believe in a Guardian Angel before, then she did now. The stupid risks she'd taken that day! Had Graham been watching over her, directing her to that church?

'Slow down on this blind bend,' he'd said. 'When the sun's low in the winter, it can catch you out.'

'I'm only doing twenty,' she'd snapped. Funny... the things you remember.

She'd probably passed the church a thousand times on the way to the supermarket, overlooking Lake Windermere. She had no idea what the denomination was, wouldn't understand the differences if she did. In truth, Nell hadn't taken too much notice of God throughout her entire life, and like a huge percentage of people only attended church when it was time for a wedding, a christening... or a funeral.

On this drab autumnal day she'd swung in, leaving the car unlocked and badly parked, and made her way to a broken bench in the graveyard. Other than the red leaves fluttering from the trees, everything was a shade of grey, as if her entire life had been bleached of colour and she'd lifted her eyes to the pewter sky, searching... for what? Bereft of words, she'd sat in silence but perhaps her soul was praying without her knowing, or maybe she'd inadvertently called for help and God *had* been listening. He'd brought her to a place - both in the physical and the spiritual sense - where she was willing to let go and simply *believe*.

Nell left that cold churchyard with a different mindset, as if something, or *someone,* had reached down and caressed her soul. Whimsical? Maybe, but there was no other way she could describe it and since that moment she wore this gift of strength like an invisible cloak, as if enfolded in the arms of a father and nothing could tear her apart in quite the same way. She was still sad, *oh yes*. But she could function, she could learn to heal.

Kath bustled into the room with a tray.

To her dismay, her daughter looked teary. Actually, she looked worn out, but Christmas could do that when you had family pulling in different directions. Jim worked long hours but like a lot of men, seemed to think that this entitled him to fall apart at home and switch off. Kath had confided in her about an affair he'd conducted a couple of years ago, and she'd been horrified that her daughter had wanted to stay married to him, but it wasn't her place to say, so she'd just listened. She wondered if Jim suspected any of this unspoken solidarity, as he was especially affable. Oh, he'd always made her welcome, kissing her on both cheeks and telling her how lovely it was to see her but he seemed edgy today. He went to unload her car and came back inside with her bags, rubbing his hands. 'More snow forecast.'

'Well, it's lovely and warm in here, I feel blessed.'

Jim carried her case upstairs and she began to empty the bag of presents she'd bought, sliding them under the tree with a deep sense of satisfaction. Adam came to say hello and she hugged his skinny frame. Such a quiet, sensitive young man. He'd spent a lot of time with his grandfather, bird watching and the like. Later, when Kath and herself were settled around the fire, Jim poured them both a sherry. There was the usual nonsense on television, and Jim began to flick through the channels in that annoying way men do. A live carol concert seemed the only programme that wasn't either for children, or a repeat. Adam didn't want to watch James Bond, and sloped upstairs.

'That's a first,' Jim said, grabbing the remote control again. 'May as well switch it off, then. I don't want the bloody God-botherers on, that's for sure.'

This wasn't the first time Jim had voiced his disdain at anything religious, but it was the first time Nell had felt a stab of irritation at such pig-headed ignorance. She didn't like the way he spoke for everyone else in this respect. 'Well, I'd like to listen,' she said, perhaps with more venom than she intended. Her remark had Kath and Jim exchange a look of mild surprise.

'Not like you, Mum.'

'What isn't like me? Some of the prayers and readings can be quite uplifting. It's the real Christmas message, after all, isn't it?'

'If you say so,' Jim said, and turned up the volume.

'You don't believe in Christian love, Jim?'

'Not especially. All that turning the other cheek and loving thy neighbour? If I had my way I'd tell that twat of a bloody farmer to stop spraying muck on a windy day,' he said, a tad belligerently, then laughed to himself. 'I could love some of the other neighbours though, especially the blonde on the quad-bike.'

'It's not meant to be literal,' she said. 'It's not down to you to go shooting him, that's all.'

'Or having sex with them,' Kath said quietly, and Jim threw up his hands. 'For goodness sake, it was just a joke.'

She had no idea how long Adam had been hovering, but he came back into the room and perched on her chair-arm with his laptop.

'I found the meaning of those Tarot cards for you.'

'Not this again!' Jim poured himself a drink, an angry nerve twitched along his jaw as he swallowed it in one gulp, then poured another. 'Cheers everyone! I've got me some real Christmas spirit.'

Adam began to read, *'You've been passive and immobile for too long and you're about to be taught a lesson. Something will come to a crisis point and you'll be forced to re-examine your beliefs.* Basically, Dad, you're between the Devil and the deep blue sea.'

'Devil worship, that's what that's all about; all those bloody cards should be burnt.'

'Ah, so if you believe in the Devil… then you must believe in God too. Or, at least you have to admit that there's a higher order than you.'

'The only order higher than me is my twat of an absent boss, an overpaid faceless corporate busy-body who's never graced the office in over two years and takes no interest in any of his employees,' he went on, draining his glass yet again, then swinging it around. 'Oh, he turns up for the office Christmas bash though, never one to miss a free nosh is Eric.'

Nell didn't like his tone one bit. This was Jim at his belligerent worst, even Adam rolled his eyes. 'Good and evil exists, yes?'

'Of course good and evil *exists*, I just don't believe it's controlled by anyone other than myself.'

'Your conscience, you mean?' Nell said, feeling that inner strength embolden her to speak. 'So, God and the Devil are inside each and every one of us and whatever has supremacy at any one time, or whatever we draw on will guide our hand? So we rise and fall by our own deeds, like karma?'

'I've no idea!' Jim said angrily, and marched from the room.

Adam closed his laptop with a definitive click.

Kath

She left them arguing - it was par for the course at Christmas, wasn't it? Besides, that remark Jim had made about turning the other cheek, was irritating. Bloody cheek! Wasn't this exactly what he asked her to do on a daily basis? She escaped to her sanctuary to sort out food for the big day. The kitchen was bathed in a gentle glow, provided by the soft lighting fitted beneath the cream wall units, and she breathed a sigh of satisfaction. Seven of them for dinner this year, including her newly divorced sister so she'd ordered a twenty-pound turkey, but when she saw it in the flesh, she wondered what she'd been thinking. Its sheer bulk, its plump legs crossed and tied, its hollow innards and the plucked skin, made it look faintly disgusting. Adam, would likely ask for a supermarket nut-roast. Her mother would only manage a sliver and yet… there was something different about Nell. She seemed so much more like her old self, although goodness knows where that little speech had come from. Jim had got all irritated as usual but then Adam knew how to wind him up.

A niggle at the back of her mind about the Tarot cards returned with a vengeance. Something didn't quite add up there, but knowing Jim, he'd left his present-buying to the last minute and Adam had almost caught him out so he'd said the first thing that came into his head. Maybe he'd been in that new-age shop where they sold artists materials and joss sticks. She'd dropped enough hints about paints and clay. This was because she'd joined a pottery class. It was a bit cliche really, living in the rural outback and making horrible pots no one wanted, but now that Adam was at university she enjoyed the social side of it as well as learning a new skill. Jim had laughed at her first attempt and it *was* horrible, so she'd put it in the garden. If it survived, she'd maybe plant something in it next springtime. No, the best part of the group was how it brought her into the village community in a way she'd not enjoyed before. She'd made two new friends. The woman who ran the pottery class seemed so lonely, soulless almost. And a man in his late sixties, recently bereaved. He had no children and seemed to find it difficult to talk about his personal life but he was so sweet, charming.

In a moment of charitable, impulsive madness, she'd invited both of them for dinner. It was only a meal, after all. And it wasn't as if they were complete strangers, she'd known them for, well… almost six weeks? She hadn't told Jim, frightened as time had worn on, that he'd create a fuss. He came in and slid his arms around her waist. 'Early night? I fancy a Christmas cuddle.'

This meant something else entirely of course, and her body sagged with sudden tiredness, like someone had thrown a switch. Her reticence was entirely psychological. Two years ago, her husband had had an affair. He'd suddenly confessed to it, one evening. He'd cried real tears; taken all the blame and begged her forgiveness. She'd tried to get past it, but their relationship had never really recovered. At the time, she hadn't asked for any details, because she knew then that it would haunt her every waking hour, although it already did in a way. Double-thinking what he'd said, wondering where he'd been. In truth, she punished him on a daily basis. 'Is that different to an ordinary cuddle?' she said, automatically.

'Oh, yes. It's a cuddle with bells on, is a Christmas cuddle.'

'I need to get the kitchen sorted,' she said, pulling out serving dishes and the frosted wine glasses. 'I don't want to be trapped in here all day tomorrow.'

He started to empty the pots from the dishwasher while she went to and from the dining room, setting the table. A huge billowing linen tablecloth first, followed by cutlery and glasses, crackers and candlesticks, then a huge shallow glass bowl which she'd found in an antique shop, saved for such an occasion. She half-filled it with water, added some tendrils of ivy from the garden, then six floating tea-lights. 'Help' must have been a token effort on Jim's part because by the time she'd done this to her satisfaction, he'd gone upstairs. She went into the pantry and carried out the overflowing crate of organic vegetables and began to scrub and peel, dropping them into a pan of cold water. On the stroke of midnight, church bells sounded across the snowy fields.

She'd gone to a service last year, alone of course. It had been a strange Christmas without either of her parents around, and in the wake of Jim's confession, not a happy time. At first she'd been dismayed to discover the readings and the hymns were in Welsh, but in the end it didn't matter. She'd never heard the bible spoken in Welsh but it was so powerful she'd sat mesmerised, even though she didn't understand a word of it. Jim had been scathing on her return, as expected.

'Feeling self-righteous?'

'No. Beliefs don't make you a better person. Behaviour does.'

He'd bought a holiday as a Christmas present. It was presented to her in a golden envelope on Christmas morning, with a glass of champagne. No sign of any clay or paint. Was it terribly ungrateful to have preferred some art materials and a cup of coffee instead? Two weeks in Cancun, leaving mid-January. She didn't know what to think about this but of course she was gracious in front of everyone, although her face must have dropped like a stone. It didn't seem like a present chosen for her. It was Jim who liked the heat, beaches and girls in bikinis.

'I hate flying,' she said.

'I've booked three middle seats on the flight so we can spread out, less claustrophobic for you.'

'Why Mexico?'

'Why not? We can relax in the sun, have some *fun,* like we used to.'

This was delivered in an unfriendly tone, as if the loss of fun was down to her not being able to move on, but then perhaps that was simply the truth. The atmosphere was enlivened when Julie arrived with a gorgeous man in tow. Her younger sister had scooped the lot in the looks department, she was a veritable man-trap with a keen sense of fun, and this was despite her marriage having ended rather abruptly after fourteen-months. They'd grown apart, she'd said, with a dismissive wave of the hand, and that was that. This made her wonder if she and Jim were simply in denial. She turned her gaze into the ice blue eyes of the delicious male specimen before her. She tried not to laugh when he was introduced as Clay.

'It's actually Damien Clayton. You can call me His Satanic Majesty, if you prefer,' he said, with a glint in his eye, shaking everyone's hand. 'But, seriously, call me Clay. My mother had an amazing sense of humour, it's no wonder I'm already something of a fallen angel.'

She laughed and said something lame about needing to switch the oven on.

Julie followed her into the kitchen and closed the door behind her, her eyes shining. 'What do you think?'

'He's gorgeous! Honestly, the sleek black hair and those lilac eyes.'

'So you don't mind him tagging along for dinner? If it's a problem, we'll clear off but we were rather hoping to stay over as well, pretty please?'

'No, no that's fine. Don't take him away, I've got plenty of food here, even accounting for the two extra singletons,' she said, forcing lemon and chestnut stuffing into the turkey.

'Oh, who might they be?'

'A couple of friends from pottery class.'

She wasn't certain but she thought Julie rolled her eyes, which was rather rude. She struggled to lift the turkey into the oven while Julie watched and quaffed wine, clearly on cloud nine and unable to function beyond fluttering her eyelashes.

'Funny thing is,' her sister went on, 'he's almost *too* perfect, you know? I keep wondering what's *wrong* with him, there'll be something, I just know it.'

'Oh, well we all have our cross to bear in that department.'

'Meaning?'

'Oh, you know, the usual. How's the job hunting going?'

'Well, I got offered something last week, but I don't think I'm going to accept and anyway, Clay's loaded so what's the point?'

'You can't do that! Anyway, what job is this?'

'Cox and Balls… the solicitors, on the main road? Imagine answering the phone?' she said, then assumed her telephone voice. 'Family law? Certainly. No cock-ups guaranteed. Speak to Mr Balls today for easy payment terms.'

Kath tried to laugh but it was too close to home. If she made a conscious effort to forgive *and* forget, then maybe their marriage could be saved. It was Christmas, after all. Their destiny was in her hands.

Julie

When the bank where she worked as cashier was taken over by the bank where Clay was Head of Foreign Investments, she'd fallen under his spell in a matter of hours. It wasn't as if she'd premeditated any of it, but her new boss had been too much of a temptation. Their affair had been sexually charged from the second they set eyes on each other. The final straw was when they got caught together in the safe. She'd been suspended, then sacked. Clay had managed to get out of the situation by persuading her to confess that she'd been stalking and seducing him for weeks. It hadn't helped her case in that she'd been caught on camera bending over the safety-deposit boxes in her bra and suspenders, and Clay had only loosened his tie.

'No point in us both losing our jobs. Help me out here, and you can move in with me, how about that?'

It was a no-brainer. Clay had two homes; a swanky apartment in London within walking distance to the Bank of England and a property on a private island in the Maldives, right on the equator. She hadn't seen either of these yet, but she was more than happy at the company apartment in Chester where he was currently doing business. He was incredibly well-connected, flew first class all over the world and gave her more spending money than she knew what to do with. Did that make her terribly selfish and shallow? Probably, but so what? It hadn't done Clay any harm, he had success written all over him and she loved hanging onto his arm… and his bank account.

She found a vacant chair by the fire in the sitting room and pulled out the gossipy magazines she'd brought, hoping Nell wouldn't start getting all sentimental about Dad. Actually, her mother seemed a lot more on the level this year.

'Are you not helping Kath in the kitchen?' she said, peering over the top of the Guardian in her steel-rimmed spectacles, a glass of sherry on the side table.

'There's nothing to do.'

'I'm sure there must be something! It isn't fair, she's running herself into the ground in there while we all sit in here, drinking and talking.'

'She loves it. Proper little Christmas angel she is.'

'Well, I'm going to see what I can do to help,' Nell said. She folded up the paper and slapped it down. If looks could kill! But then Clay winked at her and all was well with the world. He and Jim were talking about money; the root of all evil. It was Clay's favourite subject, but then he worked in finance so it would be. He looked seriously hot when he was animated, whereas Jim just looked old, paunchy and sad. He was even long-faced over the gifts they'd bought. Clay had suggested a bank account for Adam, and casually deposited a few thousand in it. Adam, rather than be excited like most normal teenagers, seemed pensive and suspicious.

'Adam, lighten up, it's Christmas,' she said to him. 'You must have a wish-list. Go on, you only live once.'

'Says who?'

'Oh, I dunno, the man in the moon?'

Still, that hollow-eyed stare. Seriously, the lad needed a good shake.

A tentative knock on the door around six heralded one of the secret dinner guests, and proceedings livened up when one of Kath's singletons turned out to be Jim's elusive boss; Eric Watson-Brown. She didn't know who was more shocked when his full identity became apparent. The job of taking his coat and offering him a drink fell to Nell, while Kath and Jim had a long, hushed conversation in the kitchen.

'Well, this is a wonderful coincidence,' Eric said, nursing a large gin and tonic. 'Nice place Jim and Kath have got here. Fancy your daughter joining the same pottery class as me, eh Nell? Big heart she's got there; my first Christmas alone, you see. Lost my wife after a long illness.'

'Really? How long have you been a widower?'

'Oh, a year and a half? I joined the pottery class to meet people. I've bought a little cottage out this way, you see, for when I retire, next year.'

'How interesting. And yes, I *totally* understand.'

Their conversation droned on. They sat side by side, talking about their respective bereavements, then it was the bloody war years when Nell and Graham had moved to Windermere, and then it was all about Eric trying to sell his bungalow in Guilden Sutton. As soon as she could excuse herself, Julie slipped upstairs to get changed for dinner. She grabbed a bottle of Prosecco and two glasses from the kitchen first, ignoring Jim's dirty looks. Kath was making gravy but it was obvious they'd had words. Hopefully the party atmosphere would get going when they'd all had a few drinks, otherwise it was going to be excruciatingly boring.

She'd brought the backless red dress with the plunging neckline, heels, the works. It matched Clay's red tie. She couldn't help wondering if it was a bit over the top for a family dinner, but Clay loved it. Maybe she'd not wear any knickers underneath either... a touch of Christmas spice! That should liven-up Jim's fusty old boss! She hung the dress, still in its dry-cleaning sheath, on front of the wardrobe. The diamond and ruby necklace - a spectacular gift from Clay - sat waiting in its plush box on the dressing table. Full of excitement, she ran a deep bath. There was oodles of hot water and she tipped half a bottle of Chanel bath elixir into the cascading water. Well, it was just sitting there at the side of the bath and it was doubtful Kath used it.

She was disturbed by Clay stealing into the room, looking for her.

'Well, well, this is where you are,' he said, and helped himself to Prosecco. Then he sauntered into the ensuite bathroom and knelt at the side of the bath, trailing a finger languidly through the bubbles. 'I'm feeling dirty.'

'Better get in, then.'

He began to strip off and she lay back, admiring his well-endowed physique. The water slapped right up the sides of the bath when he climbed in and she shrieked when he suddenly grabbed her ankles and pulled her into a submissive position. Vigorous sex in an overfull bath was like love on the high seas and it was fun - at first. They always climaxed noisily at the same time but the fully tiled bathroom seemed to make it echo as well and then the bath seemed to tilt backwards and she slipped under the bubbles. Clay laughed and pulled her up, coughing and spluttering.

'Oh, my God, I think the earth actually moved!' she shrieked, then realised why. When the bath fully collapsed, it only fell off its inch-high Queen Anne legs, so not much of a deal really but the water did go everywhere. They both climbed out gingerly, horrified at the mess. She did her best to mop it up with more of Kath's posh towels while Clay lay doubled-up with laughter on the bed, wearing nothing but a foam beard.

'You look like Santa.'

'Santa? Do you realise if you move the letter N from its cosy position in the middle of that word to the end, it becomes… *Satan?*'

'Ho fucking ho!'

She'd not laughed so much in a long while and only managed to stop when Jim banged on the door to say there was water dripping through the light fitting in the hall, and what the hell were they doing in there? He wasn't pleased when he saw the mess. No, actually he was livid and kept grumbling that it was Christmas Day and why should he be the one pulling up floorboards and trying to re-seal pipes?

'Oh. I don't know what could have happened.'

'I do!' he snapped, this time from somewhere beneath the bath. 'I know exactly what's happened, because we could all hear you in the sitting room.'

'Oh… oh, *dear.*'

Jim

He managed to fix the bath temporarily. When he made his way to the utility room to put the tools away, he discovered Kath still crying as she busied herself over the hob. He'd given her both barrels about inviting two strangers into his house without telling him till the last minute. Watson-Brown, what a bloody shock. Who wanted to sit opposite the managing director trying to eat Christmas dinner? He'd have to be careful what he said now, so much for sinking the single malt he'd been looking forward to.

In the middle of all this, Julie had marched in and taken a bottle out of the fridge, bold as brass.

'Did you see that?' he said to Kath, once Julie had drifted back out again. 'She didn't even ask.'

'Yes, I don't know what the hell's got into her.'

He did now, he knew exactly what had got into her. He'd had to sit listening to her and that obnoxious jumped-up arrogant twat of a boyfriend, humping in the bath while his mother-in-law and his boss sat sipping gin and tonics in the sitting room. He could maybe stomach Eric, since Nell appeared to have commandeered him, but that boyfriend of Julie's was something else. When they both appeared again, Julie was dressed up to the nines in the most shocking dress, spiked heels digging in to the expensive eastern rugs. She sat opposite both him and Eric with her legs flopped open in an unfeminine sprawl, a second bottle of Prosecco clutched in her hand.

'Oh… I *say*,' Eric said, and quickly averted his eyes.

Clay materialised with two glasses, a post-coital smirk on his face and a small cigar smouldering at the corner of his mouth.

'I'd rather you didn't smoke in the house,' Jim said, inwardly seething.

'Chill, old man.'

How soon could he throw him out? He was searching

for the right words when Adam marched in and returned the Christmas money to Clay and Julie. He simply threw the passbook down on the coffee table in front of them. 'I'm sorry, but I don't want this.'

'Why not? Think of all the stuff you can buy.'

'I don't need any *stuff*.'

Clay's mercurial eyes flicked over Adam and he made those inverted comma signs with his fingers. 'Services, then?'

'That's enough,' Jim cut in. How much more repugnant could this guy be?

A resurgence of the fear that Adam might say something more about the incident outside Carol's house suddenly had his pulse pumping. Of all the bad luck, to get caught out like that, when he'd been on the verge of finishing it. Not that Carol was going to let him, but he'd deal with that after Christmas, somehow. He'd been weak, he'd made the same mistake again but that was all going to change. He desperately needed Kath on side, and knowing she was busily trying to make a meal for them all was struck with an overwhelming desire to put everything right between them. If only she'd soften and meet him halfway none of this mess with Carol would have started up again but if he went down that road he was in danger of blaming her. When he examined this more closely, it was Adam and Nell who'd pricked his conscience, both of them had this ability to function as a solo entity, and he wanted some of that confidence for himself.

Maybe it was just the festive atmosphere and when it was done and he was faced with January he'd be craving cake again. But no, he had the Mexican holiday this time, like a big bright promise shining in the sky. Feeling virtuous already, he went to see if he could help set the table or something, but it was already done. In the kitchen, he began to stack the dishwasher and clear the work surfaces. Kath stopped stirring something on the hob and stood in his way, touched his arm.

'Jim, I want to apologise about the extra guests, not saying anything to you was silly, childish. And I must seem ungrateful for the holiday.'

'No, no, all my fault. Not your scene, I realise that now, but it was the pots, you know, the pottery thing? I'm sure there was an option to see some Aztec ceramics.'

'Oh, I'm so sorry, I just didn't think. It's a great idea actually. Now I've had time to get used to it, I really want to go.'

'Honestly?'

'Yes, and you're right about fun. I mean, it's all very well working hard to live in this palace of a house but it doesn't feed the soul like love does.'

'That's a bit deep.'

'I want us to have a fresh start, can we? I'll promise to stop punishing you, if you promise to stop feeding my insecurities.'

'Come here,' he said, and pulled her in close. 'I've no idea what you're babbling on about but it sounds good to me. I do love you. Just don't shut me out.'

She nodded, eyes brimming. 'Merry Christmas, Jim.'

'And a *happy* new year, that's the important bit.'

They held each other, swaying together like couples do for the last dance. Never had he felt so empowered, even his boss was no longer an irritation. And would it really do any harm to have him friendly with his mother-in-law?

'So who's the other mystery guest?' he said, nuzzling her hair. 'Am I allowed to know?'

'Don't worry, no one from work, no one you *know*,' she said, and disentangled herself from his arms with a smile.

Feeling blessed, he took the shellfish starters through to the dining room and summoned everyone to the table while Kath nipped upstairs to freshen up and get changed. Julie was terribly drunk by then, falling over the rugs and falling out of her dress. Clayton helped her into a chair, with his nose practically buried in her cleavage and his hands all over her backside. Jim opened the fizz and went round all the fluted glasses, managing to dredge-up a benevolent smile. Eric was showing Nell his state-of-the-art hearing aid. Jim couldn't resist lifting the tablecloth in order to glimpse parts of his sister-in-law he'd never seen before. She had wandering hands as well, gravitating towards Clay's upper thigh at every opportunity. It was a bit of an eye-opener in more ways than one, this relationship she'd cultivated with a millionaire sex-God.

Kath emerged and taking her seat next to Nell, unrolled her napkin with a flourish. She looked composed in a new dress, and she'd pinned up her hair. He made a toast, thanking her for the meal and everyone raised their glasses and began to pull crackers. It was only when Kath said they wouldn't wait for the missing guest that he even realised there was still an empty chair at the opposite end of the table, but the food took all his attention. The prawns and scallops were lightly spiced and juicy, resting atop a bed of crisp lettuce and drizzled with something creamy and delicious.

'Lovely food, Kath,' Eric said appreciatively, and there was a murmur of agreement.

When he was clearing the plates, the doorbell rang. He heard both Kath say hello and merry Christmas and there was some laughter at the bucket in the hall. Kath made introductions, said something about her running the beginners pottery class. It was her voice he recognised first, dark, husky. And then her perfume, dark, husky. 'Oh, do you realise, you've lost an earring?' Kath said.

'Yes, it's been missing since yesterday. I've looked everywhere.'

They came into the kitchen and he straightened up from stacking the dishwasher and his blood turned to ice. Carol stood there in a long black velvet dress, with a purple affair over the top of this with sleeves like trumpets. She extended an arm for a handshake. Mercifully, Kath was otherwise engaged, fussing with Adam's nut-roast in the microwave and looking for cranberry sauce in the fridge.

'This is Carol who runs the pottery group, Jim. Get her a drink will you, love?'

Nothing would come out of his mouth, nothing. He must have gone through the motions, must have made it back to the table and looked at his plate of dinner. He must have looked pale and shocked because Kath caught his eye and mouthed, 'Are you alright?'

He nodded and gulped down some water, then fanned his face with a table mat. The room felt unbearably hot. Kath went to open a window and Nell said yes, it was on the warm side. Warm? He was burning with fever. He could barely swallow a morsel let alone his Christmas dinner, and he'd looked forward to it all day. What the hell was Carol playing at? What sort of twisted coincidence was it that she ran Kath's bloody pottery class?

'Don't cook for myself, so this is wonderful,' Eric said, indicating his plate. 'In fact, it's better than the company Christmas meal we had in Chester, eh Jim?'

'She's a good cook is Kath,' Nell said, helping herself to roast potatoes. They smelt divine, or at least they had done when his appetite was still engaged. Now though, his guts churned and his brow felt clammy, a cold sweat running down his body. There was a moment of contemplative silence when the table seemed busy with hands, serving dishes and topping up of glasses. Adam was staring at his nut-roast, hands in his lap, then he stared across the table to Eric.

'Is that where Dad won the Tarot card reading, during the meal in Chester, last week?'

'Eh? Speak up lad,' he said, tapping his ear. 'Not so good in company.'

'TOMBOLA. Dad won the Tarot card reading?'

He frowned at this and shook his head, then asked Nell to repeat it.

'No, all the managers had a bottle of single malt if I remember rightly. Tombola? Reminds me of the village fete that does, sawdust and cheap trinkets wrapped up in a bit of paper. Don't know where you've got that idea from.'

'What *is* tombola?' Julie slurred to Nell. 'I knew a Tom once, he had a terribly small-'

'Horn?' offered Clay.

'It's a *raffle*,' Nell said, killer stare in place. 'I think it originated in Southern Italy, usually played at Christmastime.'

'Prizes are symbolic,' Adam said and Eric smirked. 'I don't think the W.I. of Guilden Sutton understood that concept. Won a bottle opener once.'

'Like Adam said, it's symbolic,' Nell responded, and everyone laughed. 'Oh, this dinner together is such a lovely idea, Kath, I'm so glad I came.'

'Me too,' Eric said, looking appreciatively at Nell like they were a match made in heaven.

As soon as he could escape, he collected everyone's empty plates, hiding his untouched dinner beneath a napkin. In the kitchen, he scraped the uneaten food into the bin quickly, trying to think of a convincing story about the tombola but his mind was a blank. There was a loud burst of laughter from the dining room, a welcome buffer to his anxious clattering and stacking. He sensed Carol behind him and the hairs on the back of his neck stood to attention. He could smell her scent, that damp mushroom smell of the house and centuries old dust.

He wiped his hands, using the towel like a tourniquet. 'What the hell do you think you're playing at?'

'I just thought, if you couldn't come to me, then I'd have to come to you.'

'Kath and I are trying to make our marriage work.'

'I won't be thrown aside like a common whore,' she said, menacingly. 'The cards have spoken. Tombola? You're a joke.'

'No, this psychic nonsense is the joke.'

'I'm your destiny, Jim. Start believing.'

She dumped some side plates on the drainer, and carried the Christmas pudding into the dining room. His hands were shaking. This was ridiculous, he needed to take control of the situation. Stuck between the Devil and the deep blue sea, Adam had said. Well, we'll see about that! He poured himself a glass of whisky and, legs shaking, took his seat at the head of the table, a slack grin on his face. Kath was hunting through the sideboard, looking for matches to light the pudding while Julie swamped it with a glass of warmed cognac. Now the room was cold. Or, maybe it was just him, because no one else seemed affected.

'So you didn't win the Tarot card reading from work, then?' Nell said.

Shit! They were still on about it.

'Tarot?' Clay said. 'What cards did you get, Jim?'

'Don't you read the Tarot, Carol?' Kath said absently, as if they were merely discussing what brand of coffee she bought.

'Sometimes, but they do need to be read by an expert.'

Clay licked his lips. 'And that's you, is it?'

'Well, I'm more qualified than most. I'm a medium,' she said, to which Julie responded, 'Then I must be a large.'

More hysterical laughter, mostly from Julie. When she overbalanced backwards off her chair Clay lifted her back up in such a way that her dress rode well above what would have been her panty-line. He expected Nell to have a meltdown at this but she was squinting at Carol as if she'd had some sort of epiphany.

'What a… what a coincidence,' she said, then unfolded her spectacles and ferreted about in a tiny pocket on her cardigan.

Adam said, 'There's no such thing as coincidence. It's the universe, trying to tell us something.'

Clay sneered. 'I've no time for the pacifists of this world, they neither change nor achieve anything.'

Music, that's what they needed, lift the atmosphere, change the line of conversation. The CD player obliged, already loaded with some loud rock music and Eric's hearing aid began to protest, like a pod of distressed dolphins. It was a good distraction but then Kath said if they had to suffer Whitesnake then could he at least turn it down? As the pounding bass line faded to a background hum, Clay settled his mercurial gaze onto Eric and Nell as they fussed with the hearing aid and three different pairs of spectacles, with the sort of intensity more suited to a mass-murderer.

'I think all the ugly people, and everyone over the age of fifty should be put to sleep, then my eyes wouldn't be offended, and we wouldn't have to put up with this inerrant squawking.'

Nell, looked over the rim of her bifocals like a startled rabbit. Kath was still opening and closing drawers, looking for matches, unaware of the tension. Carol rose slowly to her feet, diminutive, and all-powerful. 'There's an evil presence in this room.'

'You seriously dabble in the occult, do you?'

'Can we not lighten up?' Eric said nervously, 'Let's play a game. We could play the W.I. version of tombola.'

'Fuck that,' Julie said, and slumped face-down into her plate.

Carol locked eyes with Clay. 'It's *you*.'

'Takes one to know one, love.'

'I'm not your love. I'm your hate.'

'Even better. There's a fine line between love and hate, don't you find? Have you ever wondered what happens when you remove the line?'

She turned then, and her eyes bore into Jim's like a laser. 'You're *dead*.'

The floating tea-lights in the glass bowl flickered and expired. The two silver candelabra, positioned at either end of the table also hissed out for no good reason and the tablecloth ruffled with an invisible draught. Jim had an overwhelming need to find the lamp he knew was behind him on the sideboard, and he fumbled for the switch, but nothing happened.

'Must be a power failure. All those outdoor Christmas lights. Council tax'll double next year, you watch.'

'No need for artificial light, the moon's bright enough,' Adam said.

Kath, her head down in the sideboard said something about the moonlight being magical. *Christmassy*, was the word she used. Nell, intent on rooting through her pockets, even in the dim light, suddenly produced Carol's missing earring. There it was, glinting on her palm for all to see.

How the fuck had that got there? Thank fuck all the lights had fused.

'I found this in the logs, yesterday,' she said, studying Carol, and then she looked down the table, he could feel the unmistakable weight of accusation, as if she were looking right through him. Bile rose in his throat. He leapt to his feet, bumping the table and spilling drinks but it dislodged her arm and she tutted as the thing flew onto the floor. Mercifully, Kath was still slamming drawers and saw and heard none of this exchange.

'Has anyone got any matches?' she said, hands on hips. 'Let's flame the pudding before you go messing about with the fuse box, Jim.'

Clay produced a lighter. As a form of distraction from the errant earring it was perfect but there was a price to pay. It performed like a flamethrower. The pudding was a ball of fire in seconds, angry flames leaping at the suspended light fitting.

'You *stupid…*'

The linen tablecloth caught fire, sparks catching the debris of crackers and paper hats in its hungry wake. Julie screamed and leapt up, woken from her drunken stupor when a spitting ember landed on her arm. Eric, dithering, said something about the fire extinguisher he'd spotted in the kitchen but couldn't remember where he'd seen it.

'Jim! Do something!' Kath shouted, pointing to the obvious problem. She began to help Adam flap at the worst areas with napkins soaked in the ornamental floating candles. 'It's taking hold. I can smell the table smouldering.'

'That's the heat of desire,' Clay said, still sitting there as if nothing was happening, his eyes riveted on Carol.

Carol laughed, head thrown back, big loose breasts jiggling beneath her robes. A range of emotions erupted in Jim's nether regions and then the stupid woman glanced over at him lasciviously, in full view of Nell. His mother-in-law visibly stiffened. 'Dirt rises to the surface, eventually.'

'Steady-on, Nell, what's happened to all that Christian love you were spouting yesterday?'

'Don't you dare patronise me, Jim. Even Jesus wasn't a doormat.'

'Jesus was crucified,' Clay said, and held up his paper crown at arm's length, flames curling around the edge. Seriously, this guy was mental, in fact they both were, him and Carol. There's no way either of them were staying in his house overnight. Galvanised into action, he went into the hall and grabbed the bucket of water still collecting drips from the bath overflow, marched back in and sluiced it across the table. Even in the soft moonlight the room was not a pretty sight - frightening to see how the flames had taken hold after a matter of some forty seconds while they were all gaping at it. The light fitting was melted, the table was indeed scorched, and some of the carpet was pockmarked with black burns, but it could have been so much worse. His house could have burnt down!

'You… *get out!*' he snarled at Clay, then turned to Carol. 'And you; you can leave my house as well.'

Not much of a protest from anyone concerning this, even

Kath. She was more upset about her dinner-party being spoilt and bemoaning the damage, rather than be concerned about Carol and Clay driving home on icy roads, befuddled with drink.

'What about me?' Julie wailed at Clay.

'What about you?'

The arrogant bastard strode outside to where his Porsche was embedded across last summer's roses. Julie followed, beseeching him to stay, until the silly bitch threw herself down across the lane. He would have helped Adam, Kath and Eric persuade her to come back into the house, but it was an opportunity to search for evidence and so pretended to tidy-up while everyone was watching the pantomime outside. The dining room yielded nothing other than charred crackers and miscellaneous rubbish but to be sure, he crawled over the entire ground floor on the pretext of checking fuses and so on, but even Nell's cardigan, flung over the back of her chair was a no-show. His mother-in-law, watching this frenetic activity, pointed out bits he'd missed and passed him a dustpan and brush where she deemed it appropriate. After a while, he was convinced that Carol must have picked up the earring after all.

The debacle outside didn't take long to resolve and they were soon all piling back into the hall, bringing dirty snow and ice with them. Adam and Eric had their hands full, supporting a buckle-legged Julie, who was barely able to walk. Her knees were cut and bloodied and her dress had ridden-up around her thighs. Kath was trying to tug it down over her backside and pull it up over her boobs.

'It's like she's possessed!' Eric said, panting with exertion. Both he and Adam dumped Julie on the sofa, and then the sobbing began in earnest, and she was the centre of attention again. Jim double-bolted the front door, but not before he spotted Carol through the spy-hole. The moon and the stars rendered the night as bright as day, and he watched her looking up at a row of crows on the telegraph wires above the fir trees. Mad bloody bitch.

Nell had made tea.

They listened to the crump of doors closing, and then cars reversing. The lights came back on. The Christmas tree twinkled.

He found the goodwill to offer Eric a room for the night, which was gratefully accepted. Nell gave Julie a good talking too. Eventually, everyone retired to bed and he allowed himself to relax. He'd learnt his lesson alright. To be more bloody careful! And if he was going to lie, then he'd better have an explanation which added up. Hopefully, he'd never have to see Carol again. He'd forbid Kath to have anything more to do with that pottery class. And as for Adam, with his supercilious smile, he'd get a talking to tomorrow as well. He had another thing coming if he thought he could play mind games with a cloakroom ticket. No, and it was pure coincidence that Carol and Eric had turned up. The only regret was his Christmas dinner, lying in the bottom of the bin, although he felt sure Kath would oblige with another in a couple of days.

By the time he'd climbed the stairs, it was too late for Kath to start discussing anything, and given the amount of booze they'd put away, it was doubtful she'd remember every detail of any conversation, all those odd coincidences and the dirty looks. In their bedroom, he was mightily relieved to see she was already asleep. He undressed quietly by the light of the moon and placed his watch soundlessly on the dressing table. The flight tickets to Mexico were propped against the mirror, a strand of errant tinsel dangling across the envelope.

In bed, he lay exhausted, tummy rumbling and with a nagging headache, but that would pass. The important thing was, he'd managed to divert impending disaster and take back full control of his destiny. They all thought they were incredibly smug, hiding behind their Gods and their Devils, but he'd proved them all wrong. He allowed himself to gloat at his incredible fortune, turned over and closed his eyes, a twitch of contentment on his lips.

Luna, suspended in a cold sky lent an eerie bluish hue to the slowly freezing snow, and illuminated the room. It lit the single silver serpent dangling from his wife's ear-lobe as she lay wide-awake watching the moonbeams dance on the wall. And it shone across the tickets to Cancun.

Three seats, middle row. 6A, 6B, 6C.

Home for Christmas

Deck the halls with boughs of holly. Fa la-la la-la,
la-la la-la. Tis the Season to be jolly…

Home; after yet another failed relationship. Worse than that
- home alone - since her parents had flown to warmer climes
for their regular three-month winter holiday in Spain. At
least there wouldn't be any more awkward questions from
them, but that didn't include the rest of the village. The
postman spotted her outside her parents' stone cottage,
desperately trying to reverse her squealing Honda into the
almost vertical space they called a drive. He was gesticulating
with an imaginary steering wheel like men do when they see
a woman trying to park. She pretended she hadn't seen him,
bumped lightly into the garage door then ratcheted up the
handbrake. She struggled to get out, grabbing the door as it
swung violently downhill.

'Hello Pip, home for Christmas, are you?' postie said.
'You nearly took the paint off that gatepost. Good six inches
clear on the other side. You should have straightened up,
right hand down at ten-to-three.'

Whatever. So the locals still thought of her as *Pip*. When
she'd escaped the village she'd reverted to Philippa and *Pip*
set her teeth on edge now, like going back in time; although
coming home was like going back in time. Had it been the
Lake District and not a Welsh backwater, she might have

found herself checking Postman Pat's van for a black and white cat. He certainly had the same bloody enormous nose. She fumbled for her old house keys, anxious to get inside and whack the heating on.

'Hello, Daffyd. Er, yes. *House sitting.*'

'Boyfriend on his way?'

'He's had to attend a very important business conference. Overseas. Urgently, at the last minute,' she added, hoping Father Christmas wasn't listening.

'I heard the airport was shut, bad weather.'

'Oh, he doesn't rely on public airports.'

'Got a private jet has he? Or a helicopter? That's what I'd have.'

'Absolutely.'

She finally stumbled in through the front door with one of her smaller cases and a shoulder bag. There was a whole car-load of stuff on the drive, including a case of wine and a vat of chocolate products, but she didn't want to draw attention to any of that, not with Daffyd watching her every move and hovering in the porch. 'Your mother said he worked in Burger King. Had a promotion, has he? Been fast-tracked to the top?'

Damn and blast it, how many more bloody questions? 'No, no that's his much younger brother.'

'I thought he had an older brother?'

'He has lots of brothers and sisters, all different ages, dozens of them in fact.'

'Fancy that. Your mother kept that quiet.'

Satisfied for now, he handed over a slim bundle of mail and climbed back into his van. Instead of a pile of festive cards full of good wishes and letters from long-lost friends, invitations to parties and events, she was left holding the local newsletter, two official-looking pre-paid brown envelopes and *two,* just *two* tiny white ones with crooked second class Christmas stamps on them, and a rain-smudged address. What had she expected? Her parents hadn't planned on being around and none of her friends knew she was here, and anyway, it was a sign of the times, everyone did electronic greetings now. Well stuff that, what about tradition? She ripped open the cards first. One from Auntie Beryl - roses and kittens, and the other was a glittery reindeer from an old school friend. Honestly, did they not get the message after thirty-two years? She didn't do flowers, cute or sparkly things, never had. It was irritating, that they couldn't even choose a Christmas card based on known preferences, but this was surpassed by the feeling they had her down as a spinster already. She slotted both cards into her parents cardboard festive wheel above the fireplace, the only nod to Christmas in the entire house from the looks of things. There was a tree somewhere, she'd have to hunt it out. There was no way she was sitting feeling miserable for herself, knowing Christmas was packed away in the loft; except she *was* miserable and anyway, she wasn't certain as to the location of the ladders. Stuff it, then.

She wandered through to the kitchen. The brown envelopes revealed a utility bill for Dad, and a dental check-up for herself. She was still registered at the local surgery, another reminder that her relationships were too fleeting to even bother changing doctors and dentists. Six months. They hadn't even managed the seven-month itch before they'd gone off each other and Ryan elected to live with his older brother - his *only* brother - owner of the eclectic Rainbow Cafe. He must have been desperate to get away from her, since the brothers didn't get on well and Teddy had a distinct penchant for matronly clothes and voluminous floury aprons. He also owned cats, which Ryan was allergic to, but then he played football for the local team and coupled with the home cooking, the entire package had clearly been too much of a lure.

'People will talk,' she'd said to him.

'No, they won't. This isn't the country. They won't bat an eyelid.'

He was right, of course, but it still felt like a horrible rebuff, to be passed-over for a middle-aged transvestite, even though she knew this wasn't the bald truth.

The newsletter consisted of a diary of village events. She clamped it to the fridge door with a magnetic sheep and scanned the contents. Church services, her old primary school Christmas fair... *Last orders for hampers from the farm shop is Friday 12th December. A walk around Aber Falls. Please contact Will Jolley for details.* Good grief, it couldn't be. Not the same Jolley Willy; that know-it-all spotty geek of a head-boy from school? He'd been in the final year of secondary with her sister, just as she and Daffyd had started in the first year. What was he doing back here?

The last she'd heard he'd married into a wealthy family... what was her name? Amanda Knott-Browning, although she must be triple-barrelled now. Mrs Jolley-Knott-Browning. Didn't they have twins seven months after the wedding? She could never remember their names... her mother called them Pinky and Perky. *Retro night at Y Beddol December 22nd. Deck The Halls, a play by Gerald Gaultier opens December 23rd. Story time in the library on Christmas Eve will be an hour earlier followed by carol singing around the tree in the square: if it is wet then this event will be held in the hall. (No wet umbrellas to be left on the floor in the foyer as it dulls the varnish).*

That was it. From the faceless buzz of London's city life to the nosy neighbourliness of a dead-end rural village, in less than six hours.

Comfort food, that's what she needed. She hefted the box of luxury products from the local farm shop into the kitchen, to realise she'd not had the foresight to buy milk, bread or baking stuff. It was tempting to live entirely on chocolate, wine and specialty coffee, but she had a craving for mince pies. While she waited for the fridge to get cold and the house to warm through, she tramped up to the village square and considered her options. She needed a job at some point but the village was unlikely to yield anything; the lack of employment being the main reason for upping sticks in the first place and throwing in her lot with Ryan. Now that she'd returned on a semi-permanent basis, she was thoroughly depressed by the deserted streets. The main thoroughfare was like a wind tunnel, full of creaking shop signs and mostly empty premises, one of which was especially disturbing after dark, containing row after row of dusty Victorian dolls dressed in traditional Welsh costume, faded boxes of Welsh fudge and an impressive number of dead flies.

The square consisted of a handful of shops, standard bed and breakfast places, an art gallery owned by Cadw and the decaying school hall. It was a struggling community, at least grounded by the industrious guest-house owners and the hill farmers, clinging to what was left of their heritage, although they were unable to sell even sheep fleeces these days unless it was to one of those obscure cottage industries, like knitting sweaters for premature penguins. The cost of a man's labour had all but stripped the industry dry, and grumbling about it all in the pub - the one with the real ale which refused to serve food - was a major pastime for the older generation.

She bought ready-made pastry and a jar of mince, virtually home-made pies.

In the warm fug of the kitchen, as she cut-out pastry circles she imagined grinding the fluted cutters into someone's face. No, that wasn't kind at all. It hadn't all been Ryan's fault, she'd grasped at straws; both romantically and otherwise and he'd eventually worked it out. A blob of filling in each pastry circle and three lots of patty tins went into the oven. She poured a glass of wine and flicked through the local paper. Predictably, there were just two positions available in the immediate vicinity; a temporary post after Christmas for help with lambing and calving (caravan provided). A trainee bee-keeper, and a part-time cleaner for the primary school. Recalling the smell of the school toilets had her close the paper and drain the wine.

She began to scrape the fruits of her labours from the kitchen worktops. Outside looked like a snow globe, shaken hard and set down on an uneven surface, sleety rain trying to turn into full-on snow and swirling fast in every direction. Where the long cottage garden petered out onto the open hillside, there was an ancient pair of standing stones, which looked like a couple of broken teeth coated in icing sugar. Not so much standing, as leaning and lopsided, sunken and pitted with years of wind and rain. As a child, she'd pretended they were magic, especially at Christmas. Well, it had worked out like that for her sister, but not for her. Just discernible through this maelstrom of weather was a robust male figure, jogging across the skyline towards the stones in a black tracksuit with a black beanie pulled down to his eyebrows, an exuberant spaniel bounding ahead. As they approached she could hear him calling the dog repeatedly, but it speeded up then disappeared, nose down with its stump of a tail waggling, under a hedge and into next door's garden.

The man followed in aggressive pursuit, hopping over the old sagging fence, knotted with bramble and nettles. 'Martin… *Martin!*'

When she heard scuffling at the door she snatched it open and a muddy brown and white spaniel shot inside. William Jolley materialised soon afterwards, chronically out of breath. 'Sorry about this,' he panted. 'Blasted dog!'

He pulled off the hat to reveal sweaty blonde hair and wiped his forehead on an arm. There was a significant tear on his inner thigh and he inspected the flap of material with a gloved finger. 'Look at that. Barbed wire, the scourge of the countryside.'

She ignored this because the fence was supposed to stop people and dogs from getting into the garden, and secondly, she didn't really want to look at Will Jolley's hairy thigh at such close quarters. She hunkered down and fussed the dog instead, who was eyeing the empty custard cream tin.

'Friendly dog, is he yours?'

'Belongs to my parents. I'm looking after him while they enjoy a Christmas cruise.'

'He seems at home here. Went straight to the tea and biscuit area.'

'I think your folks have a soft spot for him.'

'Ah. Well, he's out of luck, they're away too.'

'It *is* Pip, isn't it?'

'Philippa Lewisham.'

'Bit of a mouthful that, I think I'll stick with Pip.'

'Fine. I'll stick with Willy.'

'Good choice. I er… hope you don't mind me saying, but I can smell burning.'

She grabbed the oven gloves and rescued the pies, sensing his hazel eyes on her floury backside as she moved around the small kitchen wondering where to put the first hot batch, the blackened pie filling spilling over the sides like molten toffee. 'Ouch!'

'Have you made all those for yourself?'

'No, course not. Visitors will be arriving all week, and Ryan loves them. Christmas entertaining, endless isn't it?'

'Postie told me Ryan's gone up in the world since he left the village.'

'In a helicopter? Excuse me…'

He laughed politely and moved various sundry items quickly out of the way for her as she slid hot trays into the only space available. 'I'm never sure if he's pulling my leg. Anyway, if you do manage to find a spare window on Friday afternoon, there's a walk-'

'Around Aber, yes, I saw. Organised walks are usually all the odd bods and the village singletons, aren't they?'

'Not at all. And anyway, you can always bring Ryan.'

'Not his thing. He's more of a pumping-iron sort of guy. Village life bores the pants off him.'

'No point asking if you want a small part, in the play then? Someone always drops out at the last minute.'

'Deck the Halls?'

His face lit up. 'You've heard of it? It's Gerald's latest project.'

'I've just read about it, that's all,' she said, 'and it's the West End for me or I'd rather not bother.'

'That's what Amanda says, although if she can find a babysitter I think she may well come along.'

'Look, I'm really busy, so if you'll excuse me?'

'Right, well, I'll leave you to it in that case,' he said, and clipped a lead onto Martin's collar. 'There's a meeting about it in the Beddol tomorrow night. If you change your mind.'

'I doubt I'll have the time, but thank you all the same.'

She bundled him out through the front door, then caught sight of the Wicked-Witch-of-the-North in the hall mirror. It was worse than she'd thought. Floury sticking-up hair, a bright pink face and an outfit comprised of thick purple leggings, a short stretchy skirt and one of her sister's ancient sweatshirts with Duran Duran emblazoned in a fetching applique across her bra-less chest.

There were three pubs in the village, five churches of varying denomination, and a much painted and photographed ancient stone bridge arching across a foaming river. On the outskirts, there was a successful bijou hotel run by two perfectly pleasant homosexual men both of whom bore the constant brunt of local gossip, perpetuated no doubt by the fact that one of them waited on tables wearing snakeskin winkle-pickers. Then there was Gerald Gaultier, the bearded-hermit-man who made life-size bronze sculptures. Some of them, dramatic figures in slightly risque poses could be glimpsed from the road, towering above his untidy hawthorn hedge. Rumour had it that he only came out to give advice to the local amateur dramatic group, or to hunt down a willing woman.

She wasn't sure what propelled her along to the pub after all, a mix of sheer boredom and a nagging need to apologise to Will; not only about her curt disposition but also to come clean about Ryan - he didn't even own a car let alone enjoy the disposal of a helicopter - before it all got out of hand on the village Internet. And even if it was just for her own morale, she needed to get out of the hideous purple tights she'd found in her old wardrobe and prove she owned some grown-up clothes befitting a mature woman. Twelve hours of navel-gazing was quite enough, especially when it was relieved only by chocolate-topped mince pies and alcohol. At least Y Beddol, the one remaining okay pub in the village, had made an effort for Christmas. Red tinsel framed the windows and a string of intermittent fairy lights trailed through last summer's hanging baskets, highlighting a handful of brown geraniums.

Gerald's red sports car was parked outside. GER 1. A curl of smoke escaping from the chimney promised the comfort of a real fire. She paused with her hand on the door and memories of where she'd met Ryan with all his big ideas, came back to haunt her. All eyes were on her as she walked in, some nodding of heads and lifting of hands in recognition. Other than the return of Will Jolley, nothing had changed in the few months she'd lived in London. The familiar sticky wooden cladding on the bar, the same men leaning against it. She could hear Gerald's booming voice and a chorus of disagreement in response. Out of the corner of her eye, Will lounged on one of the spindle-back chairs, a pint of lager in front of him. He was surrounded by the

Conwy Valley Amateur Dramatic Society; a melting pot of retired arty sorts, some of them with the kind of inflated ego which refused to accept any sort of criticism. Comments about performance were taken personally and made for violent, albeit entertaining conversations in the pub. Some of the older Welsh inhabitants, the more staunch chapel-goers, saw the entire group as positively sex-mad and virtually practicing the work of the Devil. It didn't help that Gerald did his *utmost* to perpetuate this image at every opportunity.

Martin was the first to recognise her, trailing his lead across the heavily patterned carpet, pausing only to hoover-up crisps, then Will, looking round for the dog, spotted her slow progress wobbling towards him with a glass of Chardonnay and an overflowing pint.

'Pip! Over here. Martin come away... *Martin!*'

Some poor man, probably called Martin, almost leapt out of his chair. She apologised, then sidled onto the end of a church pew on the periphery of the group. Since there was a lively on-going discussion about Deck the Halls, she was mostly inconspicuous and could study Will at leisure. Not only had he filled out but his taste in clothes had improved, Amanda's influence maybe. He thanked her for the drink and complimented her on the crushed-velvet dress she'd managed to slide into. It actually belonged to her sister but was old enough now to look retro and it fitted her rather well. In addition, her cutting-edge super-sharp bobbed hairstyle was looking slightly less sharp and much softer after five weeks away from the Scissor Happy Salon. Her natural mousy colour actually looked pretty good with the plum dress.

'I feel I should mention that yesterday I was in a very bad mood, and a public display of my special baking outfit wasn't conducive to restoring my humour. Sorry I was so rude.'

'Oh, I liked the baking outfit. Aren't you too young to remember Duran Duran?'

'Yes; but I think Simon Le Bon was quite fit, before he got old and ran to fat.'

'Married a stunning model if I recall.'

'Yasmin.'

'Fancy you knowing that.'

'My sister was obsessed, well beyond the age deemed appropriate. I found a whole load of embarrassing stuff in her room.'

He laughed at this. 'Cressida doing well is she?'

'Oh, you know Cress.'

'I did, yes. She was a honey-pot at Uni. Never short of a date if I recall but she was very focused, came out with a couple of degrees.'

'Yep, she scooped the lot.'

Her sister had indeed done very well for herself. Cressida Lewisham now owned half a haulage company, wrote history books for children in her spare time and somewhere along the way had managed to produce three gifted daughters, two of them musical and one of them strutting on a catwalk somewhere in Milan. She was married to a conductor - the orchestral version, not the bus type - owned a full-time nanny and a stunning pile in the Oxfordshire countryside. Philippa had always felt completely overshadowed, and she knew full well that sibling jealousy was often at the root of her fabrications, as she preferred to call them. To compound things further, Cressida was actually one of the nicest people and would happily offer her younger sister a job in her company at the drop of a hat. The problem was, she could never let go of the metaphorical hat, let alone drop it. Philippa never made it to university, even though her parents had budgeted for the opportunity, imagining no doubt that she'd be as clever as her sister. No, what really lay in her heart was love, marriage and children, although she'd die before ever admitting this to a living soul.

'So, what brings you back here?' she said to Will. 'It can't be the job opportunities or the eclectic night life.'

'A post that kind of fell at my feet at an opportune moment. Assistant head-teacher at the local primary.'

'Our primary, here?'

'One and the same.'

'I thought you had a hot-shot job in something commercial?'

'I did,' he said, looking down momentarily into his pint. 'I hated it, so I went back into teaching. How about you? Still in marketing?'

'I'm having a rethink. Got a few irons in the fire, it's just a case of which direction to go in, after New Year.'

'I see.'

He nodded sagely, then handed her Martin's lead so he could get to the bar unhampered. His rear view in black denims and a dark brown shirt looked pretty good. Her eyes fell on the worn suede jacket draped over the back of his chair. She just couldn't bring herself to tell him the entire truth, it was too embarrassing. She'd left a job in a local call centre, full of excitement to be moving to London, new boyfriend on her arm. The village had even thrown them a leaving party. The reality was that she'd fallen straight into another job in a call centre, trying to sell appointments for hearing aid specialists. There was talk of a promotion and the money had been good, but then it needed to be since London was incredibly expensive and she was doubtful her vocal chords would ever be the same again. Shouting on the phone for eight hours a day meant she didn't want to talk until bedtime. Ryan, had just never wanted to talk at any time of the day or night. She'd developed a form of sign language which suited them both until she'd decided to end the charade altogether and admit they simply didn't have a relationship. The relief had been indescribable; admitting to the venture as a complete failure, was rather more difficult.

It had failed for Ryan because she earned more money than he did, and he was clearly uncomfortable about that.

It had failed for her because it soon became clear that they both wanted different things from life. In a way, those few months in the city had compounded what she already knew: Ryan was not husband material. She didn't need a fun drinking partner no matter how loyal and good-looking he was and she certainly didn't want to be the breadwinner. She could hear her friends and her mother cringing, probably for different reasons, but even so. Cressida had been on the phone straightaway.

'Mother told me. Oh, I liked Ryan,' she said. 'We were in the Rainbow Cafe the other night and he looked so sad.'

'He was like that when I was with him.'

She hated that wheedling condescending tone her sister could take sometimes, as if she were lucky to get a man in the first place. It was the same tone she'd used when they were handing out musical instruments at school. Cressida managed to procure a trendy flute. Not only did it sound great, but hauling it on and off the school bus was never much of a problem. When it was her turn, there was only a double-bass left due to cut backs and all the popular girls bagging the flutes first. At least they shared the same hourglass figure, although the carry-case was like a huge carbuncle, banging into her legs. Sometimes she carried it on her back, like a snail.

'You'll be able to play in the local folk festival with that,' her sister had said, and that was more or less the death toll.

She half-tuned in to the heated conversation on her right. A tall willowy woman in some sort of theatrical costume, ash blonde hair twisted into a towering Grecian-style affair, leant across the table. 'Yes, I hear what you're saying, Gerald, but I don't agree that Holly would wear such an outfit and straddle all those men. She's meant to be an old-fashioned girl frightened to admit her true feelings.'

Gerald, bear-like and loud at the best of times, thumped the table. 'You're talking a pile of *horse*-shit, woman! She's a ball-breaking company director by day and a secret porn star by night. The whole thing's metaphorical.'

The woman's powdered cheeks flushed a deep red and several people looked across at the mention of a porn star. She plucked a moth-eaten fur stole from the back of her chair and settled it around her bony shoulders. 'That's all very well but I'm afraid from now on, I shall only be accepting classical parts. You'll have to find another Holly Harmon,' she went on, and slapped a well-thumbed copy of the play onto the table. 'Not all of us need to shout and be thoroughly offensive to make our point.'

'What? Speak up, you petal-voiced pedant! No one can hear you in here, let alone at the back of the hall.'

'Gerald… are you listening? *I quit,*' she said.

He roared like a lion poked with a stick, and flung a glass of single malt down his throat without flinching. In full throttle, Gerald was formidable, not someone you'd pick an argument with. Even Martin lay down as flat as he could, eyes fixed on Gerald's ancient sandals. Will returned with drinks, eye-rolling at the departing figure. 'Please… don't tell me?'

'When is this play going live?' she said, and his shoulders drooped. 'Next week.'

'Oh dear. Which character are you, then?'

'I'm just the prompt. There's very few male characters. It's Gerald's baby after all.'

'Ah… And if I were to be interested in helping you out here, would I have to wear the fox stole and the rouge?'

'Oh, no, would you believe that was her own stuff? It's a very…er, modern play.'

He grinned affably and in the muted light, after a second large glass of wine, he could almost pass for Simon Le Bon. Yes okay, he was quite attractive. At least she could admit that if only to herself as she weaved home, a copy of the play stuffed into her handbag.

He's betrothed, with two small piglets. Fa la-la la-la… la-la la-la.

She'd told her mother about Ryan, of course. She'd also intimated that she'd be staying in London with friends, so she was startled to hear the house phone ring and picked up tentatively. 'Hello?'

'Philippa.'

'Mum! How did you know I was here?'

'Quite simply I asked Daffyd the postie to keep an eye on the house. He told me a slightly different story to yours though. Something about Ryan and a helicopter?'

She cupped the phone under her chin and went to fill the kettle. 'I just wanted him to go away and stop prying. And he loves to rub my nose in it.'

'In other words, you were snooty and told him a lot of nonsense. Honestly, Philippa it's time you grew up.'

'Don't start, he's just as bad.'

'He plays you to see how far you might go, how many knots you can tie yourself up in.'

'Just because I wouldn't go out with him when I was fifteen. Everyone knew he really wanted to get to Cress.'

A big sigh. 'Why don't you come out here, to Santa Ponsa?'

'With all the old folks on bargain breaks?'

'Cressida's coming over for a weekend, between meetings and a Christmas Concert. If she can make the effort, why can't you?'

'I don't think so, and anyway, I've no money.'

'We can pay for the flights.'

'I heard Manchester airport was closed.'

'Cressida says it's fully operational.'

If the offer had come a couple of days previous, she may have been tempted, and she could have told everyone she'd been called away on business, but *Deck The Halls* now lay on the bedside table. Gerald's play was about the role of women in society and how lines had become blurred to such a degree that men were now as equally confused. Basically, Holly wore a shield of prickles around her heart. She longed to be a simple wife and mother but the pressures of modern society wouldn't let her. During the day she was feared and respected as a tough business woman; dominating men with a sparkly cane and an acid tongue. And then as darkness fell, she was lusted after as a porn star earning millions in front of the camera, subservient to men with a silent, distinctly more luscious tongue… but the role she really coveted, as a wife and a mother, rendered her invisible and practically worthless.

The part of Holly was made for her. She'd read it through twice, before falling asleep with a smile on her face, the lines already imprinted on her brain.

'What on earth are you going to do with yourself, home alone?' her mother said.

'Oh, this and that.'

As her mother rambled on, her gaze came to rest on the fridge door and the village newsletter. Aber Falls. Why not? The walk would give her a chance to think what to do about the play and whether she had the bottle to approach Gerald and audition for Holly. She wanted to chat to Will and find out if she was setting herself up to fail yet again but as she tried on one outfit after the other, she had to admit, it was just as much about simply seeing Will again minus the wine goggles. For the love of God, why did she always fancy men who were unavailable?

In the cold light of day, or in the cold overcast half-light of early afternoon, she spotted him with the dog at the meeting place in the car park. It was one degree above freezing, which was the most boring cold of all because there was no snow, except on much higher ground. There were children milling around, muffled up in winter hats and scarves. She wondered if Amanda and the piglets were around. Hopefully, she'd find Will a total nerd and that would be the end of that. Then he spotted her, and smiled. Oh, well… perhaps not.

She pretended to tighten her bootlaces so she could suss out the group and eavesdrop, looking over every female to see if they answered to Amanda. There were certainly no piglets in sight clinging to Mummy or crying for Daddy. They set off up the lane through the village, Daffyd up front with Will, showing him an impressive camera with all manner of lenses. There was a huge woman bringing up the rear, buttocks bumping together like a pair of over-pumped beach balls, and a man with a crazy amount of equipment, a backpack stuffed with all manner of camping gear, tin mugs and socks dangling off loops. Presently, they broke away from the road and ascended a track through a dark canopy of dripping evergreens. It was slippery underfoot and the tail-end of the river bounced alongside, spilling over the banks in bright, swirling eddies. Martin was having the time of his life and had to be called back repeatedly as he trawled the water, scattering ducks and dragging up branches trapped by vegetation.

With a bit of power-walking she managed to find herself at the front of the group. Daffyd nudged Will.

'Well, well, if it isn't one half of our local dynamic duo, joining us lower-ranking citizens for the simple pleasures of the countryside, rather than wade through her emails, attend that important conference call, or write all those Christmas cards for Ryan's many brothers.'

'All done,' she said sullenly, wishing he'd push off and shut-up. 'Needed some fresh air.'

'Ryan flies all over the world now in his private helicopter, looking for beef cattle to slaughter for burgers. Oh, yes, he's got his own helipad now - on top of the East London Burger King branch, specifically. Did you know that, Will?'

'No.'

Will's profile was inscrutable. Mostly, he stared at the folded map he'd pulled from his pocket. She shot Daffyd a hooded look, but he continued to smirk, and keep pace. Who mentioned the helicopter in the first place anyway? She'd already lost track. She really wanted to come clean to Will about Ryan, but there was no way she was saying anything in front of Daffyd. In a way, Gerald's play said an awful lot *for* her, all those feelings of insecurity and frustration with the world was epitomised in Holly's killer lines. It had to be better than admitting outright that she was a fraud.

Daffyd slowed down to take a shot of Martin as he shook water droplets from his coat, long ears slapping one way, then the other.

'About the play,' she began. 'About Holly Harmon.'

'Oh, don't worry, I think Vanessa might step in,' Will said.

This was an unexpected blow. She stopped walking. 'Well… *I'd* like to have a go, actually.'

He came to an abrupt halt then and turned to face her. 'Have you done any acting before, a drama class maybe?'

'No, nothing. I just really want to have a go.'

'What about the brassy woman in the brothel? If you can change from a basque and heels into an overall *and* handle the trolley in less than two minutes, you can double-up as the office tea-lady and nail both parts. Don't get the voices mixed up though.'

'No, I want to be Holly Harmon.'

'Look, you can't just take over the role of leading-lady in a week with no stage experience. Are you sure you even have the time for this? What with all the entertaining and so on? What will Ryan think when he finally makes it home for Christmas and you're spending every evening in rehearsal?'

His hazel eyes held hers, and it was the perfect opportunity to say something, anything… but she felt mesmerised, practically numb with a mixture of yearning. He held up a hand. 'Alright. Can you get to the school hall for seven this evening? Gerald's holding auditions.'

'Perfect. Thank you.'

He strode off, marching towards the waterfalls and she was left trailing behind, but at least she'd got a foot in the door, and now she had a plan. She'd do a brilliant audition and get the part, then spill her guts to Will and apologise for all the silly fabrications, the ex-boyfriend and the blasted helicopter. If she did it before the audition she might feel especially vulnerable and then he might feel sorry for her, or even cross, and she wanted to get the part based on nothing but passion and truth. In fact, those two keywords could apply very well to her desired future. She'd lived too long with the alternatives.

Aber Falls were in full spate and the deafening roar of the water cascading down the mountainside rendered everyone silent, except Will who was shouting for the dog, worried he'd gone into the deep whirlpool below the bridge and got carried away over the rocks.

Martin, the man from the pub, tapped him on the shoulder. 'I'm *here*.'

'Not you, the spaniel.'

'I know that's who you mean but can you please just put that bloody dog on its lead and stop yelling?'

'It's the only name he answers to.'

'But he doesn't, does he?'

'Look, I didn't christen him Martin, he's from a dogs' home and they were on the letter M.'

'Then he should have been Minty or Malty. It's a well-known fact that dogs respond better to names with an e-sound at the end.'

'I never knew that.'

The trail continued over a bridge and onto the opposite mountain via steep steps cut into the bank. Some of the families with small children turned back at this point to return to the car park, but the camping guy and the woman with the bouncing buttocks and a handful of others, looked set to continue. Philippa slogged up the path, sweating at the incline and slipping on the wet stone. She should be home, learning her lines. On the other hand, she could pursue her other project, Will Jolley. Clearly, Amanda didn't associate herself with village life so where the hell was she?

'Amanda not into hillwalking, then?' she said, breezily.

'No, not especially. There's something I'd like to tell you, about Amanda and myself. Just for the record.'

'Oh?'

'We're separated.'

'Oh, I'm terribly sorry to hear that,' she said, desperate to know who, what and why. They walked in silence, his jaw set. He had an extraordinarily handsome profile, enhanced with a faint trace of dark blonde stubble. Since he offered no further information, she played it cool and studied the scenery lest her expression give her away. Despite the bleak December day, huge swathes of dead bracken were a sea of intense russet, a startling contrast amongst the grey sky and rocks. Forests of spiky evergreens followed the contours of the hills in neat squares, and now and again they'd come across a huddle of hairy ponies and sheep. In the far distance the towering bulk of the Carneddau was topped with snow, whilst underfoot was awash with running water seeping down from the hillsides.

'I'd forgotten how pretty it can be up here.'

'It's a good stress buster as well,' he said. 'And no, you're right, she never did take to the hills. Amanda always preferred the gym, a bit like Ryan.'

Bloody Ryan. He'd never set foot in a gym so far as she knew and anyway, she didn't like all that vain, pumped up flesh. She much preferred a natural, outdoor body, tanned from the wind. As they climbed and looked back, the waterfall appeared small at the head of the valley, but gradually the ground levelled and the walking became easier. Presently, the sea glinted dully on the horizon. A police helicopter circled above, dropping through the low cloud then banking away.

'He's here!' Daffyd shouted from the back, and a chorus of laughter ensued. Oh, great, he'd told everyone.

The canine version of Martin lolloped in the undergrowth, then disappeared again, nose down. Will cupped his hands and shouted, 'Martini!'

'Oh, yes please, Mr Jolley, I'm gasping,' Big-Buttocks said. 'What a lovely idea. I don't suppose you have any cherries as well?'

She was shattered after the hike but maybe it would help calm her nerves. It didn't, so she drank half a bottle of wine instead while she paced the sitting room with a copy of the play, Holly's lines highlighted in red. What had possessed her to insist on an audition, let alone want to perform in front of an audience? Now that it was on the line her insides churned relentlessly. The short answer was that Cressida had been good at absolutely *everything* at school - except drama. She might be clever in passing exams, but she was a hopeless speaker and failed miserably if she couldn't plan anything well in advance. Singing and dancing fell into the same bracket for her sister, whereas Philippa Lewisham had always excelled at partying, especially karaoke and dressing-up. This was her chance to turn all of those skills into something respectable, and respected.

The longer answer was more complicated.

It had a lot to do with passion and truth; not only of Holly's lines and her belief in the play, but of her own search for truth too. And it had a hell of a lot to do with Will Jolley. Now that he'd admitted he was semi-available, she could admit with considerable ease that she was almost in the grip of love at first sight. What else could it be after only three days?

At ten minutes to seven, she walked the short distance to

the school hall. It was a step back in time, but it was a leap forward too when she considered that Will was now Assistant Head, and who knows what part he'd play in her future? As she neared the door, strains of Gerald's bark could be heard above a jangling piano. Inside was how she remembered it, a slight musty smell clinging to centuries-old wooden chairs and moth-eaten curtains. The stage area was newer, with a simple range of lighting and a complicated variety of scenery drops, all of which were being argued over. Will was straddled the wrong way round on a chair in the wings, a sheaf of paper in front of him. Martini, worn out with the excursion over Aber, was tied to one of the chair legs and snoring loudly. Someone called Vanessa was struggling to read the first page of Holly's lines, with Will adding in the missing dialogue where necessary and prompting her every stilted utterance. She was awful. Gerald said she sounded like a constipated donkey.

Knees knocking, she waited at the side of the stage until Gerald's black eyes fell onto hers and he motioned her to go ahead and read the first two pages. She stumbled up the five steps but then Will saw her. He smiled and nodded, told her where to stand. At the back of the hall Daffyd and Big Buttocks munched crisps and belched. The piano played the opening bars of Deck the Halls, the familiar Christmas carol version, and then faded to a long single note. This was her cue. She composed herself for a few seconds, looked past the idiots on the back row and slipped into the part of Holly Harmon without a moment's hesitation.

At the end of the piece there was total silence and she stood, caught in the footlights and blinking like the proverbial rabbit. Gerald began to slow clap, and then Will was on his feet joining in, copies of the script fluttering to the floor. It was quite possibly the best thirty seconds of her life, (not counting the time she'd won a year's worth of free chocolate). Since it was only between Vanessa and herself she scooped the part easily, but then Gerald announced to the entire hall that he was thoroughly excited by her performance and there was a hush of silence. Gerald's obsessions were legendary. She barely had chance to shoot a backward glance in Will's direction before Gerald had proffered a huge hand to help her down the steps with a gallant flourish, then pressed her against him in a tight clamp. His hands roamed over her body just within the realms of decency, his eyes boring into hers.

'I'd like to sculpt you. Something wild with cream tea-roses scrolling round it,' he said, eyebrows arching like hungry caterpillars.

'In the interval?'

He laughed, a deep sinister sound like something from a funhouse or an old-fashioned ghost train.

'I need far more time than that. Would you sit for me? I'd pay.'

'Really? Oh well, in that case…'

'And in the meantime,' he said, lowering fleshy lips to her hand. 'I'd be honoured if you'd accept the part of Holly Harmon and be present for a full rehearsal, tomorrow afternoon.'

'I accept. Thank you.'

She was allowed to escape then and walked in a state of euphoria, out into the night and along the dark road. She heard footsteps behind her and the shape of Will materialised, Martini pulling like a train towards the first lamppost.

'Pip! Wait up, can I walk with you?'

Could it get any better? This topped the day off very nicely and she tried not to grin. Leading lady in the local play and a possible love interest in less than seventy-two hours. She'd call that an overriding success. Christmas looked set to be peachy after all.

'It's only five minutes. In fact, I can see the chimney from here.'

'Long enough to say what I want to say.'

He fell into step for a minute, then they slowed to stand by the tree in the square. They both began talking at once and Will raised his hand. 'No, no let me speak first. I have to admit I doubted very much you could pull this off but you were truly wonderful, honestly you've missed your vocation. It was as if you meant every single word. I feel sure the dramatic society will snap you up as a member, if you decide to stay, that is.'

She forced her cold hands into her coat sleeves. 'Well, I'd need a paying job first, and I did. I mean, I meant every single word.'

'Did you, did you really?'

He was frowning and studying her expression with slightly narrowed eyes. This was a different kind of caught-in-the headlights but he still wouldn't let her speak. For a delicious moment she thought he might kiss her, but no.

'Ryan's a lucky guy,' he said. 'I hope he makes it for the opening night.'

'He's promised.'

'Good. I'll see you tomorrow.'

She nodded, unable to speak because her tongue felt glued to the roof of her mouth. He shortened Martini's retractable lead with a definitive snap and made to walk in the opposite direction.

Christmas week was punishing, a lot of it down to sleepless nights with endless conversations running through her mind. Some of them were Holly Harmon's lines, of course but there were an awful lot of practice runs where she was trying to say to Will that she was no longer with Ryan. The most simple of these took the form of a casual, almost blasé interaction where she simply stated that they were no longer an item after all but she was happy to stay in the village and pass up her amazing job offers without a backward glance and it was all for the best, she'd seen it coming blah blah. And the next second she was in Will's arms. Then the alarm would go off and she'd wake up and it was time for rehearsals again.

Daffyd had been roped in to play the part of the tea-lady and the woman in the brothel. This was out of sheer desperation, but it was something she and Will could laugh about in secret and they shared some cosy eye-rolling moments on stage when he inevitably got it all wrong. Gerald berated him relentlessly.

'No, no and *no!* Your delivery is all wrong.'

'I've never got a delivery wrong,' Daffyd said, hands on hips. He couldn't fold them because he'd chosen the biggest false bosom in the wardrobe department which meant he had to wear an overall provided by big-buttocks to cover it. Gerald was about to shout but his finger stopped mid-point and stroked his beard instead. 'I think you're a natural farce, Daffyd. A few funny moments to offset Philippa's serious part here could work very well. Let's continue from the scene where Holly stands astride the table in the boardroom. *Action!*'

At times it felt as if her whole life was being lived through Holly Harmon, but then she did get to spend an awful lot of time with Will.

'I don't know where you've found the time to do these daily rehearsals, what with all the entertaining as well.'

'Oh, I cancelled a lot of it, I'm having too much fun doing this.'

'Let's go to the pub tonight and order chicken-in-a-basket. They're having a retro-menu revival. You can wear that Duran Duran outfit.'

'The night before we open? Is that wise?'

'I'll make sure you get home before 9pm.'

She laughed, and then he said, 'I never knew brown eyes could sparkle before I met you, but they can.'

It was one of those compliments you could take either way. A platonic friend could just as easily make the same observation; but would they? No matter how much she ruminated, she was flattered beyond all comprehension. Of course, some of the sparkle was down to the bright lights of the stage, both literally and metaphorically, but the real glitter came from being with Will. As it happened, she was home by 10pm and sober.

Following Gerald's strict instructions, she went to bed without going over her lines again but there was no way sleep was forthcoming. The bedside lamp went on and she weighed her mobile in her hand. Will's number was in there, finally. How would she explain Ryan's no-show at the show? Maybe if she started the ball rolling with confidences, they could put their ex-partners behind them and then… It was no good, she wouldn't be able to give her best performance with all this hanging over her, and calling him was stupid when he lived down the road. Deep down, she knew this thinking was flawed. Passion and truth were all very well but which driving force would win once face-to-face with Will? They were both difficult to control.

She flung off the duvet and got dressed.

Mr and Mrs Jolley's house was a detached cottage, a few hundred yards past the pub in the opposite direction to her parents' house. It was still early, the farmer's pub must have had a lock-in because the usual unmarked police car was parked round the back. *Say no to a third caravan park* was conveniently plastered over the lower windows, so no peering in. She walked on past the school hall and there was an enormous poster advertising Deck the Halls with her name on it in tall red letters. Gerald had said that almost three-hundred tickets had been sold. For some inexplicable reason her nerves kicked in. Why then, of all times? Never before had Holly Harmon felt so close, she could practically feel the heels of her stilettos tapping into her skull like a painful mantra and a sharp nail digging into her back, propelling her along. Her pace slowed as she digested the nagging possibility of stage-fright, but she pushed on to Will's house, recognising his parents' 4x4 on the drive and a silver Audi. The rear seats were cluttered with piles of school books and boxes and there was a bath towel over the passenger seat where the dog must have sat, wet and muddy. She tapped on the obscured-glass partition of the door with her house keys. Martini barked. Presently, a light came on, then Will materialised, pausing to tie his dressing gown belt.

His voice sounded muffled through the partition. 'Pip…? What on earth's the matter?'

While he fiddled with the locks, she steeled herself to tell him calmly and truthfully that she'd dumped Ryan weeks ago and she was home for Christmas because there had been no alternative, but that Daffyd brought out the worst in her and she'd gone along with it all to save face. She'd calmly explain that Deck the Halls echoed some of her own, deepest feelings and she was hoping to make the play really shine, not only for the locals but for herself, if only to dispel the myth that she was her sister's shadow. Above all, she was sorry for all the childish lies, but now she was ready to grow up.

Then Will flung open the door and she burst into tears.

With her face crushed against Will's chest and his arms around her she was more focused on drinking in the heady spice of his recent shower, than making a confession. Her well-rehearsed speech lay cowering in some dark recess at the back of her mind. Somehow, all those premeditated words seemed entirely wrong, a real mood spoiler. She felt deliciously feline, romping in a catnip bush. There was nothing in her head, erased by the solid warmth of his embrace.

'Last minute nerves, that's what it'll be,' he said, drawing back slightly to look at her.

'Ryan's dumped me, by text.'

'What, now? Right before Christmas. By *text*? That's a bit childish, isn't it? The bastard!'

'I know. I don't care, and I'm glad he's not coming here.'

He took her hand and led her into the snug, where there the last embers of a fire in the grate illuminated an old-fashioned room, but it was cosy. Martini jumped down off the sofa and crept into his basket. Will poured two glasses of brandy and stoked the coals back to life. She tried not to concentrate on the large, framed wedding photograph hung on the wall in the recess but her eyes were drawn to the bride, over and over. A cool blonde, tall and beautiful. Her opposite in every way. Will, looked slightly uncomfortable in full morning suit.

'What horrible timing,' he said. 'Are you suffering with first night nerves as well?'

'I'll be alright, I'll fly through it with you in the wings.'

He turned and flashed her a smile and she willed her brown eyes to sparkle. There was mutual desire she felt sure, but sadly, he was too much of a gentleman to take advantage of her so quickly.

'I know it's for the best, we were never really suited. It's a shock, that's all.'

'I know how you feel,' he said, finally taking a seat next to her. 'She lied to me, Amanda did. I can't trust her anymore, despite her pleading for another chance. It started with small lies and indiscretions and that's how I caught her out. Even White lies are all very well, but who knows where it might end?'

Her heart began thumping uncomfortably, her face heating. 'What did she do, have an affair?'

'Oh no, much worse than that.'

'What could be worse?'

'I'm not sure I want to get into that right now.'

'No, no of course not.'

They sat in companionable silence, sipping brandy. There was a small tree on the plinth by the fire, decorated with a garish array of small toys and chocolates. Scattered at its base were presents wrapped in blue and pink themed paper, serving to remind her of the twins. One of each, lucky guy. No doubt he'd be busy with absent father stuff on the actual day. At least he'd got two children out of his marriage to Amanda and she experienced a sharp stab of jealousy at how this bound them together. A feeling of uneasy bitterness crept over her. She finished her drink and said something about needing to get home. He said something about getting dressed and walking her back.

'No, no it's okay, really.'

'Well, if you're sure…?'

He followed her to the door where she practically fell out into the night, desperate to be away from the scene of her shame. She ran all the way home, past the Christmas tree and the scary poster; past the war memorial and the dead-eyed dolls. There was a pop-up tent by the standing stones, and she thought she recognised the walker with the Arctic survival gear, making a fire. He'd need it if he was sleeping out there. Maybe she should offer him the garage, but what if he was a mad-axe murderer and hacked his way through the courtesy door? Or, worse than that, discovered her old copies of Christmas Bunty annuals in there?

In bed, she lay sleepless for a second time. It was a worse situation now than when she'd decided to go and talk to Will an hour ago, but that was before he'd held her and all sense had flown. It had felt so good, real. Then she'd spoilt it.

She must have slept, eventually. Waking late, she switched her phone back on to see that Will had sent her a text.

'Hope you are ok. Don't worry about tonight, you'll be fantastic.'

Hot, honest, hunky Will. He was too good for her. Nursing a mug of coffee, she watched Mrs Jones ride by on her fat, dappled cob. She and Cressida used to laugh at her. How young and selfish they'd been, how self-obsessed and cruel. Her sister had always got away with more - simply because she balanced out her random acts of unkindness by being charitable, like making cakes for the village show. Mrs Jones must be in her seventies by now and God only knew how old the horse was. It looked a bit wooden, but its ears were pricked forward as they clip-clopped assuredly towards the Spar for fags, and carrots past their sell-by. She crossed to the rear of the house and up on the hill by the stones, the tent looked like a giant amoeba pulsating in the wind. She'd camped up there as a teen with bottles of homemade sloe wine and cider. Despite the surprising rush of affection these scenes invoked, she felt alien, a fraud maybe. In London, in the faceless throng she could get away with being someone else and creating an aura of pretence, but not here in this village. Maybe this was why she was so good on stage. She needed to learn the difference though.

She let the curtain fall back and considered her plight. She'd have to grit her teeth and get through the show, *then* speak to Will and hope he'd understand. If he didn't, she'd not be able to face him ever again and that probably meant leaving the village.

The first sign that the evening was jinxed was backstage in her changing room. It was actually the old cleaning cupboard but the cast had done an admirable job of clearing some space for her costumes and fixing an old cloudy mirror to the wall. The shelves were full of bleach and other stuff and there was a smelly mop in the corner. The expensive spray of roses on her chair looked out of place. There was a card wishing her luck, from Will. Under normal circumstances this would have thrilled her. She thanked him of course and he took her downcast eyes to be those of a jilted woman, crippled by nerves.

The real beginning of the end though was when they ran

through the entire play, in full dress rehearsal and Gerald said she was lacklustre. Will said not to worry, she'd be on form for the actual live show. During this pep talk with the cast, there was a furious banging on the main entrance doors, a full twenty minutes before they opened to the public.

Eventually, Will went to see what the commotion was about, and in walked Ryan.

He did a double-take at Daffyd, hairnet, blue eyeshadow and bosoms in their rightful positions for once. His eyes flicked everywhere, seeking her out, not recognising her at first in the pin-striped suit she wore in scene one. Their eyes met. He was excited and gesticulating. 'Philippa! I've just seen the poster outside… I went to the house first. I was on my way to the pub and then I saw the poster and I thought, *wow*… she's the star of the show!'

'What the hell are you doing here?'

'Looking for you!' he said, then sighed. 'I've come to beg. Come on, it's Christmas. I haven't been able to settle since you dumped me. I'll get a better job, I'll do *anything*.'

Daffyd's mouth fell open. 'A *better* job? Geez… take it from me, mate, this one will never be satisfied.'

'Shut-up,' Will snapped, then turned to frown at Ryan. 'What's going on here? This is a big night for Pip, please don't mess it up.'

'Oh, I'm hoping to put everything right. Philippa?'

Before she could speak, Will cut in, 'I thought *you* dumped her by text, last night?'

'No, I'd never do such a thing!'

'How many brothers have you got?' Daffyd said, but every pair of eyes in the room swivelled in her direction. She stood up, even though her legs and her bottom lip started trembling but it was a now or never moment, possibly the biggest performance of her life. Acutely aware of Will watching her every move, she fixated on the boughs of holly festooned from the ceiling, twisted around the mock roof beams and hung in swathes across the stage.

'I've lied. I'm sorry everyone, and I'm sorry Ryan but I can't be with you, because I'm in love with someone else.'

There was a theatrical intake of breath and then a hushed silence as this was digested. She dared to look at Ryan but rather than feign heartbreak, he was more nonplussed, as if there were no other available men on the planet. *'Who?'*

'That doesn't matter. What does matter is that I stop lying to myself about who I am. I'm not made for London and some big hotshot job following in my sister's footsteps. I'm simply an actress, both on and off the stage. But more than anything, I don't care about equality, I just want to be with the man I love.'

She was saved by an anxious Gerald, guffawing and slapping his leg. 'She's the real Holly Harmon that's why! Get on that stage and let's knock em dead. Five minutes everyone.'

Gerald took her arm and practically frogmarched her backstage. She glanced back and caught a glimpse of Ryan and Will; they both looked mutinous.

'Channel your negative energy and all that anger, remorse or whatever into Holly's lines at the end where she breaks down, yes?' Gerald said.

She nodded glumly. That wouldn't take much acting.

When the curtain went up and the piano played the opening bars of Deck the Halls, she balked for a second at the audience. There were rows and rows of them, shuffling, coughing and texting. At first, she blanked them out, then as her confidence grew, began to draw them in to the story and make eye contact with the front row before quickly averting her eyes. To her horror, she spotted Amanda, unmistakable with that stature and the blonde hair. Every so often, this woman scanned the room and scrutinised the wings, no doubt looking for her *husband*. To give her her due, she clapped wholeheartedly at the end of every act and scene change, laughed at Daffyd when he genuinely screwed up with the tea trolley because he'd forgotten to align the wheels, and along with the rest of the audience, had tears of laughter streaming down her face when he managed to somehow fall backwards off the stage and lose one of the boobs. Someone lobbed it back on stage and she stole this moment of chaos to glance at Will seated to her right, but his head was down over the script.

He avoided her in the interval too, and then when the final scene opened and Holly Harmon threw off her shirt and tie, discarded her mini skirt with a Velcro rip and stood especially vulnerable and half-naked in a basque and high heels, she delivered her speech. Will was redundant as prompt because most of what she said were her own words.

'I may be shackled by the modern world into a female stereotype but real freedom comes from being an individual.'

A smatter of applause.

'Greer was not completely right you see, not for me. I have all the sexual freedom I want, I can survive in a man's world if I choose...' she said, then walked stage left and lowered her voice, hands on hips. 'But what if I don't choose it? What if... I choose marriage and motherhood. Should I fear scorn?'

Someone wolf-whistled and shouted, 'I'll marry you, love!'

She blew kisses. A smatter of laughter. She spoke loudly and passionately to the end and the tears were real by then, but the audience had no notion of that and stood to applause and stamp their feet. Will had already left the stage by then because she became aware of him sitting next to Amanda. His face was devoid of all emotion and his arms were crossed. Why was he sitting there, was he making some sort of stand? She'd never felt so equally elated and miserable at the same time. She found it difficult to stop crying; in fact she managed it all through the encore where the entire cast sung Deck the Halls - some of the audience joined in with the Welsh rendition - and right at the very end a suspended net above the stage released thousands of holly leaves edged with glitter. She wasn't sure about this, since she was the only cast member with bare skin by then, but Gerald came on stage with a magnificent bouquet, and a silk wrap which he draped around her shoulders. Then the entire cast except Will, joined hands and bowed and the curtain came down and the house lights went up, and that was that.

'Champagne! On me, everyone. To the pub!' Gerald said.

She escaped to the cleaning cupboard but the basque wouldn't come off by itself and so she abandoned the idea and grabbed her coat and boots. She could hear Gerald shouting for her, something about local press and a photographer. She slipped out though the fire door, unseen and walked briskly down the street towards the square. There was no way she could face Will or Ryan, or anybody. Ryan might try the house again, so on impulse she headed along the grassy track towards the standing stones. It was the place she'd always escaped to in the face of her adolescent inferiorities, parental arguments about her grades or simply being too drunk to go inside. Maybe she had truly grown-up a little because she was no longer a slave to those feelings, but maybe unrequited love was worse than all of them put together.

She leant against the biggest stone and contemplated the moon where she'd stood many times and waited for magic to show. It arrived in the form of Martini, scampering and snuffling along the path. At first she assumed he'd broken free and began to call him, but then the shape of Will materialised in pursuit. Not running this time, but walking purposefully. He drew level with her and it took all of her willpower not to touch him.

'How did you know I was here?'

He held up a doggie bag and shook it. 'I followed the trail of stardom and glitter.'

She frowned so he opened the bag, and when she looked inside, it was full of holly leaves. 'Busted,' she said. 'Sorry I ran away.'

'No, it's kind of admirable, not wanting to bask in your glory. And the basque looked amazing.'

'I wish all of that were true.'

'The whole village loves you.'

'Despite my acting, on and off the stage?'

'You confessed. And anyway, all that misunderstanding with Ryan was nothing compared to Amanda's deceit,' he said, then took a deep breath. 'The twins aren't mine, you see. I did the honourable thing without question, and now I'm having to extricate myself. Stupid of me.'

'Not stupid. Do you still love her?'

'God, no. I put her straight, hopefully for the last time. She's in the pub, getting drunk with Ryan.'

She felt the stirrings of a huge smile crease her face as the moon slid from behind an indigo cloud. She instinctively searched the ground for magic moonbeams and found herself pinned back against the ancient stone, Will's hands on either side of her shoulders. The buttons of her coat had come undone and her hair had escaped its crazy wig, but he was smiling and his eyes were dancing.

'You know the origins of Deck the Halls, don't you?' he said. 'It's Welsh of course, but the original words were in celebration of New Year, not Christmas. I think that's an important point because it's about the future.'

'What's that got to do with anything?'

And that's when he kissed her.

Jan Ruth lives in Snowdonia, North Wales, UK.

This ancient, romantic landscape is a perfect setting for Jan's fiction, or simply day-dreaming in the heather. Jan writes contemporary stories about people, with a good smattering of humour, drama, dogs and horses.

For her full list of titles please visit: http://janruth.com/

31972607R00066

Printed in Poland
by Amazon Fulfillment
Poland Sp. z o.o., Wrocław